THE
COUPLE'S
REVENGE

BOOKS BY DANIEL HURST

THE
COUPLE'S
REVENGE

DANIEL HURST

bookouture

Published by Bookouture in 2023

An imprint of Storyfire Ltd.
Carmelite House
50 Victoria Embankment
London EC4Y 0DZ

www.bookouture.com

ISBN: 978-1-83790-824-0
eBook ISBN: 978-1-83790-823-3

PROLOGUE

The abandoned warehouse on the edge of town was a grim place for the couple to find themselves. They were used to spending their time several miles away, in a more affluent area, where the buildings were well-maintained, warm and cosy and filled with things that brought joy to the property owners. Unlike this place, which was unloved, unkept and, most importantly, unused.

It was this warehouse's lack of use that had given the couple the idea to include it in their plan. This would be, they had decided, the perfect place for them to get away with their crimes, the most serious of which would result in a very long prison sentence should they ever be apprehended by the authorities.

And that crime was murder.

But at that moment, the couple weren't quite guilty of murder. They were, however, guilty of abduction and holding somebody against their will. Two crimes: they were enough for the time being, which was why the couple were taking a moment to consider the gravity of the situation before proceeding with the rest of their plot.

The pair stood side by side, their breathing hard and fast. They held hands, an affectionate gesture but more so because each needed the support of the other at such a crazy time. One male, one female.

The couple were taking their time, or at least that was how it felt to the person tied to the chair in front of them. Then again, maybe they were just psyching themselves up for the next part.

The part that involved the knife.

As the man regarded the shiny blade in his hand, the woman beside him kept her eyes on the prisoner in the chair. She saw how much he was sweating, and could hear how much he was begging for his life, not that every word was comprehensible due to the gag that was stuffed into his mouth. He wriggled, trying to break free of his restraints, ropes that were crudely wrapped around his wrists and ankles, preventing him from going anywhere with ease, even if he was to escape the chair.

But most of all, she saw something she recognised easily.

It was fear.

The prisoner was terrified.

Of course he was. He knew he was about to die. But the prisoner should have thought about the consequences.

Now it was too late.

The knife was raised, and the couple were only seconds away from finishing what they had started.

They were going to have their revenge.

BEFORE

ONE

SARA

The house is quiet, that mid-afternoon lull like music to my ears as I sit at my desk in the spare bedroom upstairs and try to conjure up the energy to reply to my boss's email. But instead of doing that, I'm whiling away a few more minutes of my working day by gazing at the photograph that sits beside my laptop. It's a photograph of the three most precious people in my life, and that is why it sits in a place where I reside for eight hours a day, meaning I get to look at it often.

The silver rectangular frame houses an image of my husband, Guy, alongside our children, Amber and Jacob. It was taken on a family holiday in Tenerife, three years ago, and the three tanned faces in the photo grin back at me as my mind drifts to the lovely two weeks we spent on that sun-kissed island during the school holidays.

As he often does still to this day, Guy is wearing a baseball cap backwards over his crop of light hair, as well as sporting a short-sleeved shirt that showcases what were once very toned arms. Slowly but surely, Guy's enthusiasm for the gym has waned over time, and he doesn't have muscles like that nowadays, though he still likes to think he does and flexes his 'guns' for me every now and again as we are getting into bed in the evening. But bulging muscles were never really my thing anyway. I find it far more attractive when a man uses his arms to hug his children as opposed to lifting weights, and that is what Guy is doing in this picture here.

His left arm is around Amber, at the time a very tempestuous fifteen year old who already, at that age, believed she was too cool to go on holiday with her parents. But there was no way we were leaving her behind and risking her having multiple house parties full of underage drinking and all manner of hormone-riddled promiscuity, so I made sure she boarded that plane to the Canary Islands with us. But despite getting off to a rocky start on that trip, Amber soon relaxed by the pool and, as the holiday went on, she turned her frown upside down and smiled for enough photos to ensure her parents had plenty of good mementos from the trip.

While Amber is not quite as difficult nowadays, at eighteen, plenty of other things have changed. She had a late growth spurt, one that saw her not only rise above me in the height stakes but, eventually, her father too, much to his chagrin. I imagine she will continue to tease him about being shorter than her for many years to come, and I'll make sure to laugh every time she does, because it is funny seeing Guy try to defend being dwarfed by his daughter. Amber has dark hair now, having dyed it from its natural blonde, which upset me a little at first, but I have got more used to it and actually think the colour suits her better. She has already told me it has made her more popular with the boys, not that I had asked, but if a change of hair colour has done wonders for her confidence, it can't be a bad thing, can it?

Guy's right arm is wrapped around the shoulder of our youngest, Jacob, who was twelve when the photo was taken and even then, as he was on the cusp of becoming a teenager, he still retained his cute, boyish looks. His button nose is wrinkled up in the picture, as it always is when he grins, and it is a grin that can best be described as mischievous. Jacob was a little whirlwind as a boy, and I certainly remember him being a bit of a handful in Tenerife as he constantly changed his mind about what he wanted to spend his time doing. One minute it was playing in the pool, the next it was going to the beach and then it might be wanting to go and play football with some of the other kids at the resort. Then there were the demands for ice cream or drinks or anything else he wanted to keep cool in the hot temperatures, and if it wasn't Guy getting off the sun lounger every ten minutes to placate Jacob's newest need then it was me. But he was always a happy little soul, as he still is now just a few months shy of his sixteenth birthday, and that's the main thing. As long as Jacob and, indeed, his sister are happy then Guy and I are happy too, because they are our world and the reason for everything we do in it.

I could stare at the photo all day, reminiscing on the past and wondering where the years of my children's lives have gone, but funnily enough, that is not what my employer is paying me for. I wish there was a high-paying job that only required me to be the best mother I could be, but as far as I know that's a job that is not compensated financially. Instead, the role that actually pays me a liveable wage is the one in which I have assumed the title of Accounts Administrator, and it's a job that means when I'm not looking at photos of my family, I'm staring at spreadsheets full of numbers and trying not to go cross-eyed.

Snapping myself out of my daydream, I force myself to get serious about this email that I'm supposed to be composing. But do I have to do it? I really wish I could say no, but because it's being waited on by Janice, the manager of the company I work for, then the answer is probably yes. It certainly is if I want to keep paying the mortgage on this lovely property I call home, as well as continue to afford to contribute towards giving my children anything they want, so it's time to put my fingers on the keyboard and start typing.

I write an email destined for Janice's inbox, and while it's accompanied by a lot of heavy sighing on my part, I say all the right things in my message.

Yes, a deadline of next Tuesday for that report is absolutely fine... It's no problem at all that I might have to work late one night this week... And I agree, I'm sure things will be easier when Becky comes back from her maternity leave.

Like the good employee I am, I've managed to tell three lies in one email, but I did it in such a way that it's well concealed and thus allows me to keep my job. The truth is that the deadline Janice has just given me is terrible and almost impossible: I'll have to work late more than one night this week to get it done; and things definitely won't be easier when Becky gets back from leave because she's more of a hindrance than a help in our workplace.

With a quick sip of coffee and another heavy sigh I click the send button. With that, Janice will get my satisfactory response.

My work here is done.

For now, at least.

Glancing at the time, I see that Jacob will be home any minute and, with that in mind, I happily leave my desk and go downstairs, grateful to be able to work from home because it allows for such moments as this in my working day. Instead of being stuck in some soulless office on an awful industrial estate, I get to operate from my house, which offers far more pleasant surroundings. Instead of chunky printers, cluttered desks and piles of dirty cups in the kitchen sink, my workspace here is much tidier. I'm also spared the attention of Creepy Colin, the overweight Compliance Manager, who always used to ogle me whenever I passed his desk back in the pre-Covid days, when we were in the office five days a week.

Quite what he was ogling at I have no idea, because at forty-five years of age and having borne the brunt of birthing two children, my body is hardly a temple any more. My figure is a far cry from the lithe and limber bodies of the younger women in my department, not that Creepy Colin ever seemed to care about that. Any female seemed to qualify for the pleasure of his lingering gaze, and I can't help but wonder what he is doing to pass his time now that he is also working from home.

Then again, with unrestricted and unmonitored internet access, I dread to think.

Entering my kitchen, I'm careful to check if the tiles have dried in here after I mopped them earlier. That's another benefit of WFH. Menial house chores can get ticked off during the week instead of being saved for the hectic weekends.

The tiles have dried, so I'm free to walk where I want to, and I make my way to the breadbin, and take out the fresh loaf inside and place it on a chopping board. Then I go into the fridge and try to predict what my son will fancy for his sandwich filler this afternoon.

Jacob might be in the final year of secondary school but that hasn't stopped me from keeping up with a tradition that started way back in his primary school days. Never one to be enamoured by the concept of education, from an early age Jacob despised having to go to school and was mortified at how many years of listening to teachers in classrooms he had stretching ahead of him. But while there wasn't much I could do to make his time in a classroom better, I did endeavour to make sure he was happy once the bell rang and school was out, and one of the many ways I did that was by making him a sandwich that he could enjoy once his education was over for another day. Leaving work early to collect him, I would always be at the gate with a smile on my face and a tinfoil-wrapped sandwich in my hands, and my little lad would gobble it up as soon as he was with me. Of course, he quickly grew to the point where he wasn't so little any more, but while his body got bigger, his appetite did too, and the sandwich tradition stayed. Jacob no longer needs me to collect him from the school gates, but he does still like to tuck into a sandwich after a busy day of Maths, English and Science lessons, and that's why I'm in the kitchen now.

One ham and cheese sandwich coming right up.

I sometimes wait for him to get back and tell me what he wants between his bread before making it, but I have to be on a Zoom call with Janice in ten minutes, so I can't dawdle today. I'm sure he won't turn his nose up at what I've prepared for him when he walks through the door any minute now. Teenage boys eat anything, as my exaggerated grocery bill will attest to every week at the supermarket checkout.

I hear a few spots of rain hitting the window and look outside to see if there is any sign of Jacob, hoping he won't get caught in another rainstorm and come home drenched like he has a couple of times this term. He'd rather that than have his mum collect him from school, which seems silly to me but makes perfect sense to him and his self-conscious teenage ways. But he's going to avoid the downpour today. I can see him sloping down the driveway towards the front door, his rucksack slung over his left shoulder and his head down, his face turned away from the dark sky above.

I speed up my sandwich making as I hear a key turning in the door, and after a blast of cold air enters the house, the door slams shut, and I prepare for my son to enter the room, ravenous and prepared to eat everything in sight.

But for some reason that doesn't happen.

'Hey! Are you okay?' I call out to Jacob as I cut his sandwich in half and drop the two chunky pieces onto a small plate. I expect he'll want crisps to go with it, but he's big enough to go looking in the cupboard for them. However, there's no response from my son, and as I glance towards the kitchen door, I see him rushing past it.

'Jacob?' I say, but he ignores me, and then I hear the sound of his feet plodding up the stairs.

I have no idea what's going on with him, but he's never come home and behaved like this, so I pick up the plate and rush out of the kitchen to try and catch him on the staircase. He's almost at the top by the time I get there.

'Hey, what's wrong? Did something happen at school?' I ask him, concerned he might have just failed a test or got a detention for doing something one of his teachers disagreed with. He's not a troublemaker by any stretch of the imagination, but everybody gets a detention every now and then, don't they? I know I got a couple in my time, mainly because I was talking to friends when I should have been listening to my teacher, but it's all part of school life, and as long as the detention is not for anything serious, then it's okay. Jacob is still ignoring me, and despite me telling him that I've made him a sandwich, he continues walking away until I hear his bedroom door shut behind him.

Not willing to let him come home without saying hello to me, I go upstairs after him and knock on his bedroom door, repeating myself by asking him if everything is okay.

'Go away,' comes the curt response.

'What about your sandwich?'

'I don't want it.'

'Really?'

'I'm not hungry.'

I find that hard to believe, because if it's true, then it's the first time in a decade. Maybe I should go inside and see him. But a teenager's closed bedroom door is a risky threshold to cross, so I hesitate, and when I check my watch I see that I'm supposed to be on my call with Janice in one minute.

'I'll leave your sandwich out here,' I say through the door, placing the plate down on top of a small bookcase in between Jacob's bedroom and my makeshift office. Then I return to my desk and pick up my set of headphones before logging on for my call with my boss, right on time, like a good employee should.

Though I'm in the meeting, my mind is a million miles away. I'm thinking about Jacob and what could have happened to bring him home in such a bad mood. I know I wouldn't be the first mother in the world to have a grumpy teenager on her hands, but Jacob has always been a happy soul, which is why I'm worried now.

I get even more worried when my meeting ends, an hour and ten minutes later, and I find the sandwich is still sitting on the plate outside his bedroom.

What's going on with my son?

After knocking on his door and failing to get any answers again, I brave sticking my head inside his room to try my luck there. All I get for my trouble is Jacob telling me to get out and leave him alone, so I do as he says, afraid to darken his mood even more by lingering.

If he won't talk to his mother about whatever is troubling him, then he will have to talk to somebody else.

This might just be a conversation for his father.

Hopefully, he will be able to get to the bottom of whatever is troubling our son.

TWO

GUY

An energetic game of 5-a-side football is just what I need after eight hours spent hunched over my desk at the office.

Life as an auditor is a lot kinder to my bank balance than my waistline, which is why I always make the effort to attend this weekly football game with a few of my friends from my school days. My oldest mates, Baz, Fruit Loop, Chuckles, Simmo (not their real names) and I decided that we could no longer keep our beer bellies at bay as we entered our forties, so after several pints in the local pub one night, we decided to call ourselves a team and enter the local 5-a-side league that operates on the floodlit, artificial pitches in the centre of town. That seemed far more appealing than trying to get back into any kind of routine at the local gym, a place I used to frequent often but have not been spotted in for a few years now, after I realised adding muscles to my arms wasn't doing as much as I'd hoped it would in staving off my midlife crisis. Now, with our team set, we play football every week against five other hopeless souls who can barely kick a ball but need to burn off a few calories, and it's all a bit of harmless fun and a welcome respite from the drudgery of our day jobs. It does mean I'm a little later in getting home every Thursday night, and while that's not usually a problem, it seems it might be this week. That's because I have a missed call and a message from my wife, Sara, and it's obvious that something is troubling her, namely our son.

You need to talk to Jacob when you get home. Something is wrong with him.

The text doesn't tell me much, so I quickly call my wife before I leave my car to join my friends, who have already started doing their hamstring stretches on the pitch.

'Hey! Sorry I missed your call. I just got your text. Is everything okay?' I ask, sitting behind the wheel of my car and staring out through my windscreen at my hapless mates.

'I'm not sure. Jacob went straight to his room after school, and he hasn't come out since. He won't talk to me either. I don't know what's going on with him.'

'Oh, okay,' I say, racking my brains for whatever it could be that might have troubled him. But he's a fifteen-year-old boy, so it could be anything from girl troubles, friend troubles, teacher troubles or just general puberty troubles.

'I've never seen him behave like this,' Sara goes on, her worry emanating through the phone.

'I'm sure it's nothing major,' I reply, trying to calm her nerves. 'Probably just a bad day at school. We've been lucky with him so far, but we can't have expected him to make it all the way to his GCSE exams without a few hiccups along the way.'

'Maybe.'

'I'll talk to him when I get back, okay? In the meantime, maybe start cooking something that smells delicious. That will surely tempt him out of his room.'

I expected my joke would get a laugh from the other end of the line, but it doesn't, which tells me Sara is even more worried than I thought. That's why I offer to change my routine slightly this week.

'I'll come straight home after the game tonight,' I say, voluntarily forgoing my usual post-match pint with the lads at the pub conveniently located opposite the pitches.

'Thanks. I'm sure he'll be okay. I'm just worried about him.'

'No problem. I'll see you soon. Love you.'

'Love you too.'

I end the call before grabbing my kit bag and getting out of the car, telling myself that whatever the issue is, it will most likely have been resolved by the time I get back. However, as I walk over to the side of the pitch, I haven't been able to shake my worries about my son, and my wife's distress, and I'm wondering if I should just cancel my participation in this upcoming game and get home sooner. But that would mean leaving my teammates a man short, and considering we usually lose when there are five of us, they won't stand much chance when there are only four. That's why I drop my bag beside theirs and jog over to join them on the pitch, where they are busy trying and failing to shoot the ball into one of the empty goals.

The usual array of banter flies around between us as we all briefly ask the others how they have been, before looking across the pitch to try and size up this week's opposition. I'm encouraged to see that the five guys we are due to play tonight all look at least ten years older than us, so maybe our fresher, more youthful legs will be the telling factor over the course of the next sixty minutes, and this might be one week that actually ends in a win rather than another demeaning 6–0 defeat.

But as my eyes wander across the five faces at the opposite end of the pitch, I see one I recognise, though I can't quite remember from where. Fortunately, Chuckles, the best man at my and Sara's wedding twenty years ago, has the answer for me and the rest of our group.

'That's Kevin Atkinson,' he says, suddenly losing his attention on the ball that was just passed to him, which ends up bouncing away from us before coming to a stop by the fence.

'I thought it was,' Simmo says, shaking his head. 'The poor chap.'

The rest of us don't need to seek further clarification about the man on the other side of the pitch, because with his name being spoken, we all know exactly who he is now. He's the father of Zoe Atkinson, the twelve-year-old girl who tragically took her own life three years ago, after being subjected to some awful bullying at school.

The story broke the hearts of almost everyone in this town when it came out. I say almost everyone because there were a few horrible people who didn't seem to care, and they were people associated with Mason Burton, the twelve-year-old boy who had been the one responsible for bullying Zoe. Mason's parents, an awful couple by the names of Dean and Tracey, were unapologetic about their son's actions when pressed for comment on them by both the school and the police in the aftermath of the suicide, as well as unsympathetic to Zoe's parents' plight as they tried to come to terms with what had happened to their daughter. Mason had been expelled from that school, which was the least that should have happened, but that was all that came of it. Mason was free to find another school and get on with his life, while poor Zoe was gone, and Mason's parents carried on as normal too, utterly unrepentant at how their son had ruined the lives of two parents just like them.

Worryingly, Mason, who is in the same year as Jacob, landed at my son's school, which resulted in me, Sara and dozens of other angry parents descending on said school to voice our concerns about that child potentially mistreating some other poor kid. The headmistress assured us they would be keeping a close eye on Mason, and I guess it's worked because it's been three years and nothing else has happened where that little runt is concerned, although Jacob did tell me once that Mason got suspended for bringing cigarettes into class when he was fourteen, which hardly surprised me.

There is no doubt that boy is trouble, pure evil if you ask me, and there is a small headstone in a graveyard not far from here that will attest to that.

It's the kind of story that would make anybody sick, but as a parent I couldn't comprehend what Zoe's parents must have gone through after seeing their youngest child end her life due to the awful actions of someone else. They spoke to the media briefly and only to ask for privacy and, as far as I know, they were granted it. I admit to not giving them much thought in recent times, but that has changed now I'm sharing a pitch with Kevin, the dad of the deceased, and as we get into position to begin the game, I can't help but find myself watching him.

He looks okay, but what am I expecting? Him to burst into tears as soon as he gets the ball? I guess enough time has now passed for him to at least be able to function somewhat normally in society, and like my friends and I use this game as a way to blow off some steam, I guess he's using sport for much the same reason.

The game begins, and I find myself on the same side of the pitch as Kevin, who, like me, is carrying a bit of a beer gut and is moving quite gingerly in the early stages. He races towards me when I get the ball, and without paying it much attention, he's able to easily tackle me and win back possession for his team.

I need to get my head in the game and stop thinking about the horrible things my opponent has been through in the past. But just like scoring a goal or coaxing a troubled teenage boy out of his bedroom, it's easier said than done.

THREE

SARA

I'm aware that staring at the front door isn't going to get it to open any quicker, but I'd rather do that than stare at my son's bedroom door because I know that definitely isn't opening anytime soon. I'm loitering downstairs and waiting for Guy to get back so he can have a go at talking to Jacob, but he hasn't arrived home yet from his football match. I do wish he'd hurry up because the longer he takes, the more anxious I am becoming.

Something is seriously wrong with Jacob. It's been almost four hours since he got home from school and he's still barely said a word to me, nor has he re-emerged from his bedroom after disappearing into there earlier. The sandwich is still untouched, and as far as I know he doesn't have any food in his room, so he must be starving by now. But he would still rather hide away than come out and face me, and that is not normal behaviour for him at all.

We're so close, me and my son. It's not unusual for us to watch a bit of television together while we wait for Guy to finish work, the pair of us helping one another answer quiz questions on the various shows that populate the channels in the early evening. Jacob always handles the sport and geography ones, while I tend to field the trickier questions like any that have anything to do with numbers. Together we make a good team, and I even joked once that the two of us should apply to try and get on one of the quiz shows. Who knows, we may end up winning a bit of cash. But Jacob shot down that idea, telling me that it would be very uncool if he was seen by all his mates on television with his mum, although he was very polite in the way he did it.

That's my boy. Polite and considerate.

And happy. Always happy.

Until today.

I contemplate having another go at talking to him, but then decide it's better to give him space for a few more minutes, until his father gets home, so I go into the kitchen and make myself a cup of tea. While I do, I can hear a few footsteps above me, which tells me Jacob is moving around in his room. I guess that's better than him lying on his bed stewing in whatever has got him feeling so down.

As the kettle boils, I distract myself from my troubles with one child by turning my attention to my other one, and I'm glad that things are not so tricky at the moment with my eldest. Amber is currently away, enjoying her first year at university, far from all the dramas at home but not too far for us to be able to go and see her and deliver emergency food rations as and when she needs them.

And based on how it's been going so far, she needs them quite a lot.

We message frequently despite the newfound distance between us, and while it was difficult to see her move out of the house when she first left, the passage of time has made me more accustomed to the new reality of having one of my children residing elsewhere. I send her a quick message now to see how she is, though I'm not expecting a prompt response, because with it being seven o'clock on a Thursday night at uni, I'm sure she's got lots of exciting things going on.

I'm glad she is settled in her new life now, and I feel super proud of her for knowing what she wants to do at such a young age. Amber is studying Criminology at University of London, which is impressive, if a little expensive; but we are happy to help out with her fees as much as possible, if it means she ends up getting a job she loves. Neither of her parents can profess to having followed their dreams, but things can be different for our children. Amber could be a crime scene analyst one day, which sounds like a grim job to me, but it's a job she has always wanted to do, ever since she used to dress up in a white coat and wander around the house with a magnifying glass when she was ten, trying to solve imaginary crimes, most of which involved ketchup that she used as fake blood. Whatever she ends up doing, I'll be proud of her anyway, just like I would be with Jacob, who has some big decisions of his own to make in the next year or two.

He'll be finishing school after his exams and will have to decide whether he stays in education or ventures out into the world of work and, the last time I checked, he was still undecided about that. All I know is that he loves football and wishes he could play professionally, something I'd love to say he has a chance at doing, but it's a tough career choice, and despite playing with enthusiasm, he may be lacking the requisite level of skills. Not that I would ever tell him that. I'll let him keep dreaming for as long as I can because I love him and only want the best for him.

That's why this situation right here is driving me mad.

I don't know what to do to help him if he won't tell me what the problem is.

Putting my phone down, because Amber hasn't replied quickly as predicted, I finish making my cup of tea and consume it over by the window, peering out through the slats in my kitchen's blinds in the hopes that I'll see the headlights of my husband's car arriving any moment now.

I don't begrudge him his weekly game of football because I know he needs the release, plus he wouldn't get much exercise any more without it. Our sex life has hardly been active over these last few years, but rearing two teenagers will surely do that to any couple. At least that is what I've tried telling myself, though Guy has mumbled a few comments recently about how we should try and make more of an effort when it comes to the bedroom and by 'we' he means 'me'.

We had harboured hopes of having more time to ourselves when Amber went to university, but, of course, Jacob is still around and, even if he wasn't, my energy levels are not what they were in my twenties. These days, it feels just as much effort to pick up the remote control and turn the TV on as it does to try and engage in a little lovemaking, so I'm not sure how Guy and I will rekindle that particular spark. I tell myself that it's not a huge issue, but Guy might feel otherwise, just like he has made a few comments about the two of us making more time for date nights again, leaving Jacob home alone while we go for meals or a couple of drinks. But while I loved date nights back when we were actually in the dating stage, these days, I'm much happier to curl up on the sofa with a good movie rather than put on a dress and pair of heels and go into town. I certainly don't have much energy for anything more after work most days, and I'm surprised Guy feels as he does because the last time we went out for a meal, he looked just as sleepy by the end of it as I did. But surely our recent 'issues' are very minor in the grand scheme of things and won't lead to any major problems between us. The way I see it, we're a team and we've been a good one at that, having raised two beautiful children while holding down careers and having plenty of fun holidays along the way.

Two kids, secure jobs and a lovely home.

That's enough, right?

I like to think so, but I do worry Guy might have an alternative answer to me.

Then again, there are certainly people far worse off than us in this world, and I'm reminded of that whenever I go online and spend a few minutes scrolling through my social media feeds. Like Janet Islington, for instance, an old colleague of mine who not only lost her partner to cancer last year, but is now having to do battle with her own form of it herself. Or Brenda Williams, a friend of a friend who ended up having to sell her house recently to pay off the gambling debts her husband had secretly accrued. And then, of course, there is the sad plight of the Atkinson family, who were torn apart when Zoe, their youngest daughter, ended her life after being bullied at school.

I have been Facebook friends with Zoe's mother, Mary, for several years, ever since Amber was in the same after-school gymnastics class as Zoe's sister, Erica. Amber and Erica were good friends, which meant I got to hear a few first-hand accounts of how the loss of Zoe had destroyed the family. But as time went by, I didn't see as much of Zoe's parents. They weren't as prominent at school events or the gymnastics classes or just in general. It seemed like they were hiding away and, after what they had been through, who could blame them? As a result, Amber didn't see as much of Erica either and that friendship gradually fizzled out. That's the thing with a tragedy like the one that ripped through the Atkinson family. It's not just what they lose in the immediate aftermath, it's everything they lose in the following years as a result of the changes in their habits that it brings about.

These days, I only see that family's movements online. Mary posts things on Facebook every now and again, mostly inspirational quotes or touching tributes written to remember people no longer with us, but every now and then she will post something a little more personal. Like today, for instance. She has uploaded a photo of herself reading a book on her sofa at home with the caption:

Ready to lose myself in another trashy novel

I think about liking the post but hesitate, as I always do when it comes to anything involving poor Mary, because simply liking one of her posts seems so insignificant when she has lost a child. But then I press the button, deciding that it might be meaningless but I can still do something, and maybe the tiny dopamine hit she will receive from seeing the notification will make her forget about her troubles, for half a second at least.

But that's enough social media for one day. I've got enough going on in my own life to be spending time worrying about other people's.

I'm worried about Jacob.

And Guy still isn't home yet.

FOUR

GUY

After promising Sara that I'd be home straight after my game finished, the last thing I needed was that game ending in a draw and going to ten minutes of extra time. Despite the scoreline being delicately poised at 4–4, I tried to tell my teammates that I had to get going. But did they listen? And did I put up a good enough fight when they insisted I stay and help them try to get the goal that might see us crowned the victors? I guess not because I'm still running around this pitch, huffing and puffing and trying to ignore the burning stitch in the right side of my abdomen.

Though ten years our senior, the team we are playing against have more than held their own, and they are clearly fitter than us, not to mention better with a ball at their feet than we are. But we're a dogged bunch, me and my mates, and we've been as determined on this pitch here tonight as we were years ago on those nightclub dancefloors when we were eighteen and desperately trying to get a girl to give us a kiss. As extra time nears its conclusion and the spectre of a penalty shootout looms large, the ball breaks to Kevin Atkinson, and he dribbles the ball towards me.

'Get to him!' Chuckles shouts, urging me to take action as the nearest defender to the attacker. Despite closing the distance to Kevin quickly, I'm hesitant to put my foot in and really try to get the ball off him, and it's a hesitation I've detected from my teammates, too, where this particular player is concerned. We all know Kevin's story and what he has been through, and thus we are reluctant, if not downright shy, about being too aggressive with him. As a result, we're being far too tentative around him, and as he dribbles past me easily, I wonder if he is aware that we're taking it easier on him than the rest of his team.

Whether he does or not, it doesn't stop him from shooting the ball into the top corner and, with that, the game is finally at an end. We've lost, I'm exhausted, and Chuckles is not happy at any of our defending over the last sixty minutes or so, but at least I can go home now and see my family.

'Cheers, guys,' I say as I make my way around the other team, shaking their hands and being a gracious loser. I've certainly had plenty of practice in my time. As I reach Kevin, I feel that awkwardness around him again, and end up simply mumbling to him instead of looking him in the eye and speaking clearly when I tell him he played well.

Kevin's handshake is quite weak, and despite doing my best not to look at him too much, I make eye contact with him and, when I do, I see that even with scoring the winning goal in the last minute of extra time, he is far from happy. There's no smile, no light, no joy in his expression. He just finishes shaking hands before trudging over to the side of the pitch and putting on his jacket.

I instantly feel guilty for looking forward to going home and seeing my family when his was left in ruins years ago. What kind of atmosphere is waiting for him when he gets back to his house? How have he and his wife been dealing with the loss of their youngest daughter? My mind immediately comes up with a few strategies that I would employ, ones that mainly involve copious amounts of alcohol; but just because my reaction to a severe loss would most likely be to drink myself into oblivion, it doesn't mean that Kevin's is.

I walk to my car with Chuckles beside me. As we reach our vehicles, I see him watching Kevin getting into his own car.

'Don't worry about not tackling him at the end there, mate,' Chuckles says quietly. 'I was going easy on him too.'

'I just feel so sorry for him,' I say as we watch Kevin reverse out of the car park. 'I can't even begin to imagine what he's going through.'

'Hell, most likely,' Chuckles says with a sad shake of the head. 'I suspect he'll never get out of there.'

We snap out of our sombre trance and say our goodbyes, shaking hands and slapping each other on the back, before he goes off to join the rest of our group as they cross the road to the pub.

I'm heading straight home, as promised, and once I have my car on the road, I put my foot down a little more than usual, marginally breaking the speed limit simply to shave a few seconds off my arrival time, so that Sara might be a little less annoyed at me. I'm not sure that's going to cut it, though, because as I park on the driveway, I see the silhouette of my wife at the kitchen window, telling me that she's been watching out for me. I guess she really meant it when she said she was worried about Jacob, but I was hoping he would have come out of his room by now.

Rushing inside as fast as my aching legs will carry me, I am greeted in the hallway by a troubled Sara.

'He's still not talking to me,' she says as I take off my trainers and try not to get cramp in the process.

'I'll go and see him now,' I reply before heading for the stairs. 'I'm sure it's nothing.'

'Make sure he tells you, whatever it is. He has to tell one of us.'

I climb wearily up the stairs, but Sara is right behind me and is still there when I get to Jacob's door.

'Am I going in, or are you?' I ask her, acknowledging how close she is behind me.

'You go. I'll listen from out here,' she whispers, like some spy on a covert mission trying to avoid detection.

But Jacob isn't stupid, and I'm sure he knows both of us are outside his bedroom now, which may not be doing much to brighten whatever mood he's in.

'Okay, here goes,' I say before knocking on the door and entering with a bravado that I hope exudes confidence, because I don't want my son to be as dismissive to me as he has obviously been to his mother. But that remains to be seen.

All I can do right now is close the door behind me, ask him what is wrong and then hope that he enlightens me.

Surely it's not as bad as my wife thinks. She often overreacts to things, things that turn out to be nothing. Let's just hope it's the same again.

If not, and there is something to finally worry about, I guess she'll get to say that famous line.

'I told you so.'

FIVE

SARA

It's been ten minutes since Guy went into Jacob's room, and I'm still no nearer to finding out what might be bothering our son. I have at least given up on lingering outside his bedroom door, though, and have gone down to the kitchen to make a start on dinner. I'd usually have a meal prepared by this time of night, but this is no ordinary night.

As I try to concentrate on slicing onions and not slicing my own finger, I hear somebody coming downstairs and am hopeful it's Jacob, coming to apologise for ignoring me all night before telling me what the issue is. But it's not him; it's his father.

'What did he say?' I ask, putting my knife down for a moment.

'He says he doesn't feel well,' Guy replies casually before reaching into the fridge and taking out the orange juice carton.

'Is that it?'

'Yeah, he's got a bit of a stomach bug, but he's feeling a bit better now.'

Guy drinks from the carton, which usually annoys me, but I'm too distracted for it to worry me right now.

'That's all it is?'

'That's what he told me.'

'And you believe him?'

'Yeah. Why would he lie?'

'Why wouldn't he just tell me earlier, if that's all it was?'

'I don't know. At least it's nothing major.'

Guy seems as if he's satisfied with this, and it's clearly case closed in his opinion. But I can't believe that's all there is to it. Mothers have instincts when it comes to their young and mine are telling me that something is seriously wrong.

'What did he say? What were his exact words?'

'He said he started feeling ill this afternoon and felt a bit sick at school, so he came home and has been resting.'

Guy must be hungry because now he's picked up the knife and has started chopping the onions I've discarded. But dinner can surely wait for a little while longer.

'I don't think he's telling the truth,' I say, basing that on all my years of experience as Jacob's mother. 'I think there's something else.'

'Like what?'

'I don't know, but it's not a damn stomach bug! I haven't heard him go to the bathroom once since he got back. And he doesn't look pale or ill or anything, does he?'

'What do you want me to say? I asked him what was wrong, and he told me.'

'And you just took his word for it? You didn't think he might be lying? Trying to hide what's really bothering him?'

Guy puts down the knife, appearing frustrated at me pressing him.

'What shall I do, Sara? Go back up there and ask him again?'

'I don't know. All I do know is that it's not a damn stomach bug, because I know what he's like when he's ill, and he's not like that.'

'Maybe he is now.'

'What's that supposed to mean?' I cry. Is my husband suggesting that I've failed to keep tabs on my son's evolution and, as such, have lost track of when and why he might be struggling with something? If so, it would just be another example of him being mistaken, because unlike him, I am always proactive when it comes to our kids, and that means I know exactly what they need and when they need it, ideally before it's too late. His motto in life, and especially parenthood, has usually been 'it'll be all right', but that just sounds like burying his head in the sand to me, because it's easier to be like that than face an uncomfortable truth.

'He's not a kid any more,' Guy tells me, confirming the point he was trying to make. 'He's growing up. He's changing. Maybe part of that is him acting differently and not needing us as much. You know, we had the same thing with Amber.'

I get the slightly brutal point my husband is making, but I don't agree with it. This is not about Jacob suddenly gaining independence overnight and wanting to be left alone to deal with a stomach bug in private. It's something more; I can just sense it, and I learnt a long time ago to trust my internal instincts, especially when it comes to my children.

'Go up there and tell him he is to come downstairs for dinner,' I say, picking up the knife myself and retaking charge of the meal prep.

'I don't think he's going to want to eat if he has a stomach bug.'

'Then he can come and take some medication for it, something he hasn't done yet, which strikes me as odd, because usually that's the first thing a sick person would want.'

'He might not want to come downstairs.'

'I don't care. He's not staying hidden away all night. I want him down here so I can look at him, and then I'll know for sure if he's telling us the truth or not.'

I take out a pan and turn on the heat before getting started on cutting up a chicken breast, while Guy wanders away, telling me he's going for a quick shower but that he'll also try and coax Jacob out of his room along the way.

I whip up the meal in record time, but my heart isn't really in it, and it shows in the presentation of the food on the plates. But the main thing is Guy has been successful in getting Jacob to come downstairs, and as my son enters the kitchen, I get a proper look at him. He looks tired, haggard even. I guess he could be ill. I still have my doubts, so I offer him a plate.

'Do you want to eat with us?' I ask Jacob, hopeful about his answer.

'Thanks,' he says quietly as he takes the plate, and while it's a relief not to have him shout at me and storm off again, it does make me even more convinced that he was lying to Guy earlier.

Who wants to eat when they have a stomach bug?

My son's appetite is clearly bigger than keeping up with any lie he might have told, but as he sits down and begins putting food on his plate, I decide not to push him too much. Not yet, anyway. I'll just let him get some food inside him and then gently broach the subject again later before he can go back upstairs.

While Jacob is still very quiet and I keep a close eye on him, the dinner doesn't pass in total silence. Guy tells us all about his football match, a tradition of his because Jacob usually likes hearing about how his dad got on in his weekly game. But as Guy gives us the rundown of all the thrills and spills from what sounds like an eventful game, I'm conscious of the fact that this week, Jacob didn't ask his father to tell him what happened, nor does he seem to be paying much attention to what his dad is saying. He's just stabbing at his chicken, moving a few of the pieces around his plate and generally eating a lot less than I would expect him to.

'I think we could have had a chance to win if we'd really gone for it,' Guy goes on, having no problem shovelling food into his mouth at a rapid rate in between all the talking. 'But we eased up on them a little bit, especially with who they had on their team.'

'Who was it?' I ask, pretending to be concentrating on my plate rather than my son's across the table from me.

'Kevin Atkinson.'

I don't need Guy to tell me who that is: I recognise the name immediately. And it seems I'm not the only one who does, because Jacob drops his fork then and it clatters loudly on his plate.

'Careful there, buddy,' Guy says, chuckling at his son's clumsiness before carrying on with his meal; but I'm not eating. I don't think that was clumsiness on Jacob's part.

I think he dropped his fork because he was nervous.

But what about?

'Yeah, it was a surprise to see him,' Guy goes on. 'But I suppose it's a good thing that he was playing football. You know, staying active, being social. Suggests he's doing better these days.'

Jacob has still not picked up his fork, and now he's pushing his chair back from the table.

'I'm full,' he says.

'But you've barely touched your meal,' I observe.

'You're not feeling well, right, buddy?' Guy says, eyeing up his son's leftovers. 'That's okay. Go and rest and give us a shout if you need anything.'

Jacob can't leave the room quickly enough, and no sooner has he made it upstairs than I hear his bedroom door close. Great, he's hiding away from us again.

'Something's not right,' I say.

'I'm sure he'll be feeling better in the morning,' Guy says before reaching across the table and picking up Jacob's plate, clearly keen to help himself to what's going spare.

'Did you see how he looked when you mentioned Kevin?' I ask.

'Huh?'

'When you said Kevin's name. He got all nervous. Dropped his fork. Then he left.'

'I think you're reading too much into him dropping his fork.'

'What if he's being bullied?'

Guy finally stops eating and puts down his own cutlery.

'What?'

'I'm serious. I've never seen him behave like this. You might believe his story about a stupid stomach bug, but I don't. I think he's upset about something. Or worried.'

'He's not being bullied.'

'How do you know?'

'Because he'd tell us if he was.'

'Would he?'

'Yes!'

Guy raises his voice then, and while it's loud enough to startle me slightly, I've at least succeeded in getting him to take this seriously.

'I'll have another word with him before bed,' Guy tells me after apologising and calming down. 'But for now, please try and stop worrying about him.'

'I'm his mother,' I say as I reluctantly go back to my food. 'I'll always worry about him.'

'Yeah, I know,' Guy admits, giving me a smile, though failing to mention that, as his father, he'll always be worried too. 'But everything will be fine, I promise.'

My husband genuinely seems to believe that, and maybe I should too. Life certainly would be easier with that outlook.

So why can't I?

Why am I feeling more anxious about my son's behaviour by the minute?

SIX

GUY

I kept my word to Sara and had another go at speaking to Jacob before we all retired to bed tonight. But, just like when I was in his bedroom earlier, I found it difficult to get much in the way of words out of my son. While it was hard work to get him to tell me that he felt ill earlier, it was even harder when I went back to try and get a few more answers. Jacob grunted and mumbled a few things about being tired and just wanting to be left alone so he could go to sleep, and I told him I was going to do that, but that extra time I spent with him did make me start to think differently about things.

And now I'm worried my wife might be right.

Something else is wrong.

It's not just a mother who has good instincts about her child. A father has them too, and despite doing my best to take my son at his word and allow him to tell me he was just suffering the effects of a stomach bug, I am aware that this behaviour is very out of character for Jacob. It's obviously not the first time he's ever been ill, but on those previous occasions he's acted differently to this. He's never been one to hide away when he's been under the weather. If anything, he's even more vocal when ill, moaning about whatever it is that ails him, pestering for pills and miracle cures and generally making a big nuisance of himself, until he starts feeling better again. He's usually such a bad patient that I often made a joke to him whenever he was telling me how much he was struggling, reminding him that 'there was many a man who had had his head blown off and not moaned about it'. Of course, it was a joke said to make my son laugh, and it always worked, even as he got older and realised how ridiculous it was. But there had been no laughter tonight, not even so much as a small smirk when I said that old joke of mine to him just before I closed his bedroom door and left him to get some sleep.

I hate to admit it, and I'll never say it out loud because I like to give off a more carefree vibe, if only to offset my partner's anxiety, but I think it is the case here.

My wife is right.

We turned the lights out in our bedroom almost an hour ago now, but neither I nor my restless partner beside me have managed to achieve sleep. I've been lying on my back, staring up at the ceiling, while Sara has been tossing and turning and generally making a tangled mess of the duvet. It's a warm night so I'm not too bothered about rearranging it so it covers all my body again. I am concerned about what might be troubling Jacob, though, and as the clock ticks past midnight, Sara lets me know she is still worried too.

'If he is being bullied, I should go in and talk to one of his teachers,' she says, suddenly sitting up in the bed as if she's just had a stroke of genius in the early hours of the morning, like a writer who wakes up with a new story idea and must jot it down on a notepad before it's forgotten forever.

'Calm down. We don't know what is going on yet,' I say, being the voice of reason, a part my wife usually plays on all matters except when it comes to our offspring.

'What if it is that? What if somebody is being mean to him?

You think he'd tell us, but I don't know if he would. He might be embarrassed. Or too afraid.'

'Let's just see how things go tomorrow. If he comes home in a better mood, then maybe it was just a bad day. He could have had an argument with a friend, for all we know. I doubt he'd tell us about that. Or maybe the girl he likes ignored him in the corridor. He definitely wouldn't tell us about that.'

'Or maybe he is getting physically or verbally abused by some thug, and he's too scared to do anything about it.'

'Sara, please.'

'No, I'm not going to drop it until I know for sure.'

'Just don't go jumping to conclusions.'

'I'm not. I'm being proactive.'

'Or paranoid.'

'What?'

'I knew I shouldn't have mentioned seeing Kevin Atkinson at football.'

'What's that got to do with anything?'

'Are you kidding? Do you not remember what you were like when that story about Zoe first came out? How you used to keep yourself awake at night, worrying yourself sick that one of the kids was being bullied and that they were going to hurt themselves like poor Zoe did?'

Sara doesn't say anything to that, which lets me know that she definitely does remember that time.

'Look, I get it,' I say. 'It was a horrible thing to happen in this town, and it scared every single parent in it, but just because it happened then, it doesn't mean it's going to happen again. The schools are more on the ball with looking out for bullying or anything like that these days. They'll nip it in the bud before it ever gets to that awful stage again.'

'We hope.'

'Well, it hasn't happened again, has it? And Amber made it

safely through school without any problems, and, so far, Jacob seems to have done so too.'

'Unless it's happening now.'

'If he is being bullied, then he knows to talk about it. We made sure to teach him that when Zoe died, and he promised us he would tell us if anything like that was happening.'

'That was three years ago.'

'I doubt he's forgotten.'

'I suppose.'

I sit up and put an arm around my wife's shoulders, offering comfort as well as a little warmth, because while it's not freezing we should think about getting back under the duvet again soon.

'I'll see how he is in the morning,' Sara decides. 'If he's better, then I'll drop it. If not, I'll phone the school.'

'Okay, that sounds like a good plan to me,' I say before kissing Sara on the top of the head and settling back down on my pillow. It's a relief when Sara settles down too, and while I don't hear any soft snoring coming from her side of the bed, I hope she manages to drift off to sleep at some point. But I find it impossible to get some rest despite a day of work and a gruelling football match, not to mention all the drama of this evening at home. I'm not sure why it is because I'm normally a good sleeper, but as the hours tick by and I find myself staring at the wall beside our bed, one image keeps coming back to me.

It's Kevin standing on the football pitch.

Seeing him has affected me far more than I first thought, and I'm finding it impossible to forget about him like I seemingly managed to forget about him once before. Maybe it's the surprise of him being there. It was the first time I'd seen his face since his photograph was used in several articles, both in print and online, not to mention all the times he was caught on camera going into his house or leaving the offices of the lawyers he had clearly hoped would be able to do something to punish the family of the bully who had forced his girl to take her life. Or maybe it's because I feel like there is nothing but sheer luck separating me from him. We're just two guys who had children, and while I've been fortunate enough to have mine make it safely through the majority of their adolescence, he wasn't so lucky. His child got snared in something appalling, and now his life will never be the same again.

Aware that it's never wise to contemplate such things as luck, death and the unpredictability of life at three o'clock in the morning, I get out of bed to visit the bathroom, hoping that a quick toilet break and perhaps a glass of water will help me clear my head, and I can return to bed in a more peaceful state. But that doesn't happen because as I pass Jacob's bedroom on the way to the bathroom, I hear something coming from the other side of his door.

It sounds like crying.

I step closer to the door to try and hear better, because I really want to know for sure that I heard what I thought I did before I enter the room, but as I do, I tread on a creaky floorboard, and the noise gives my presence away. Sure enough, any sounds from within Jacob's room stop quickly, and now I'm not sure if I really did hear what I think I did.

I visit the bathroom and quench my dry throat with a little tap water before I get back into bed. Sara asks if I'm okay, clearly still just as awake as I am, and I consider telling her about what I might have just heard out in the hallway. But I don't. No point worrying her at this time of night, and there isn't much she can do about it now anyway. As we both roll over, I decide that, just like my wife, I am going to have a close look at our son in the morning, to see if he is feeling any better. Because now I'm feeling very worried too...

I did manage to fall asleep a short time after that, and when I woke I remembered something very clearly. It was my last thought before I drifted off, and it was a very strong one.

I was thinking about how I hoped Sara was wrong about Jacob being bullied, or more specifically, I was thinking about what I'd do if anybody ever dared hurt my son.

It's simple, really.

I'd kill them.

SEVEN

SARA

I'm drained after a rubbish night's sleep, but I'm still up well before my son, and this is another red flag. Going against the grain of what most kids are like, Jacob has never been a difficult child to get out of bed. I wouldn't go so far as to call him a morning person – nobody in our family is – but he's not a sleepy nightmare either when it comes to waking up, getting dressed and getting out the door to start the day. He's usually up with little fuss and is often quite chatty over breakfast, if a little forgetful when it comes to items for his school bag or remembering where he left his blazer when he took it off the previous day. But this morning, as I had feared, he is still acting out of character. There's no sign of him emerging from his bedroom at half past seven, when his alarm is supposed to go off, nor do I detect any noises coming from the other side of his door as the clock creeps towards eight. It's obvious he's going to be late for school if I don't take decisive action, so I'm just about to enter his room and ask him why he is still in bed when Guy volunteers to do it for me.

'I got this,' he says, cutting me off in the hallway and knocking on Jacob's door before entering.

My husband has usually left the house by this time in the morning, to begin his commute across town, but I'm grateful for his presence here today because it seems like I might need all the help I can get, and that only becomes more obvious when I hear him arguing with our son seconds later.

'Hey! What's going on?' I cry as I enter Jacob's room to find Guy standing over the bed on which one very angry teenager is lying.

'I don't feel well! I'm not going in today!' Jacob cries, attempting to pull back the duvet that Guy has obviously peeled off him. But Guy keeps a tight grip on it, not conceding so easily, and this reminds me of all the times we would have the same fight with Amber when she was younger and it was time for her to go to school. But that was Amber, and this is Jacob, which means this is different. If my son was genuinely ill then I would have no problem allowing him to have the day off from school, but I do not believe that illness is the reason for his change in behaviour. And by the sounds of what he says next, it seems Guy has finally come to the same conclusion.

'Tell me what is wrong!' Guy says, and, suddenly, it's as if he is on my side after all, rather than being the one to tell me to calm down and not worry about it. I wonder what changed his mind. Possibly a sleepless night, just like I had. And then, after Jacob attempts to convince us there is nothing sinister going on, Guy explains his newfound concern.

'I heard him crying in the middle of the night.'

'What?'

I'm shocked and look to Jacob for clarification, but he is still trying to get the duvet back, though his skinny, pyjama-covered body is no match for the strength of his father.

'I wasn't crying!' Jacob protests.

'Yes, you were. I heard you!'

Guy seems adamant about it, and if that's the case, then I believe him.

'Just tell us what is wrong, Jacob, please,' I say, making sure not to shout like my husband, because the last thing our son needs is both of us playing the role of bad cop. However, that tactic doesn't work either, and after a few more minutes of fighting in vain to be left alone in bed, Jacob seemingly gives up and rises to his feet before telling us to get out so he can prepare for school.

'I don't know what is going on with you, but you better tell us when you come downstairs,' Guy says before he storms out of the room, finally relinquishing control of the duvet, and it falls to the floor beside one of Jacob's football magazines.

'Talk to me,' I say to my son as he opens his wardrobe and pulls out a white school shirt, but I seem to have reminded him that I'm still in his room, because he suddenly launches into another angry tirade, so I follow Guy's lead and leave too.

The pair of us exchange worried looks as we wait for Jacob to come downstairs, and I can tell that my husband is not only stressed about our son but also about the fact that he is going to be seriously late for work if he doesn't get going now. That's why I decide it might be better if he makes himself scarce before Jacob appears, otherwise we might soon have World War III on our hands.

Guy takes a little persuading before he's on board with the idea, and after seeking reassurance that I'll be okay to deal with Jacob myself, he finally leaves the house. It's just in time because Jacob appears soon after, dressed in his uniform and with his rucksack hanging off his shoulder.

'What do you want for breakfast?' I ask him, checking my watch to figure out how many times I might have to break the local speed limits to get him to school for nine.

'I don't want anything.'

'You have to eat something.'

'I'm fine.'

He heads for the door then, but I'd rather he didn't leave the house on an empty stomach, so I grab him a breakfast bar from the cupboard for him to hopefully eat in the car. But him leaving the house without having breakfast does at least mean that we stand half a chance of getting him to school on time.

I use the car journey to try and get my son to open up some more to me, or at least I do after it becomes obvious that he's not going to initiate any conversation himself, so while negotiating the heavy traffic, I try to negotiate with the person in the passenger seat too.

'If there is something wrong, you only have to tell us, and we can help you,' I say, my eyes on the busy road ahead but my mind very much on the person sitting beside me in the passenger seat. 'Your father and I love you; you know that, don't you? We just want you to be okay.'

'I am okay.'

'This behaviour is very out of character for you.'

'I'm fine.'

But I'm not comfortable with him going to school with this still unresolved, which is why I bite my lip and wonder whether or not I should say the word that is on the tip of my tongue. But I'll only spend all day regretting it if I don't, not to mention worrying myself sick, so I'm going to say it.

Here goes nothing.

'Are you being bullied?'

I glance at Jacob then and see him noticeably stiffen in his seat, before he turns his head to look out of the window so that I can't see his face.

'No,' he mumbles back, but it's about as convincing as the time he told me he wasn't the one who kicked the ball through the neighbour's greenhouse.

'What's going on?' I ask, pressing him because I'm sure I'm on the right track here.

'Nothing is going on. Just leave it!' Jacob says and then he does something ridiculous. He attempts to open the car door while we're sat at a red light. Thankfully, the internal locking system does its job and keeps the doors closed while the engine is on, so he can't go anywhere. But that doesn't mean he didn't just try to abandon ship in the middle of a busy road during rush hour.

'Jacob, what the hell are you doing?' I cry, exasperated at my son's nonsensical behaviour.

'Just let me out. I want to walk,' he tells me, but he's not going anywhere.

The lights go green, so I'm forced to drive on lest I risk angering the drivers behind me and they beep at me with their horns. But I'm not dropping it and continue to question Jacob all the way to the school gates. However, he refuses to talk to me any more, and as I hear the bell ring to signal the start of class, I feel like I have little choice but to do as he wishes and open the doors so he can leave.

No sooner have I pressed the button, than he flings his door open and races off across the playground, leaving me behind to watch him go, ten times more worried than I was when we left the house only twenty minutes ago. I'm not ready to leave yet though, so I park the car and head inside almost as quickly as my son, though unlike him I am not heading to the classroom.

I'm going to the headmistress's office.

Just like it always is when I've been in here attending various parents' evenings over the years, it's slightly surreal to be inside a school as an adult rather than a child. Even though it's a relief to no longer have to wear an uncomfortable and unstylish uniform, the fact I'm dressed in plain clothes only causes me to stand out – and nobody wants to stand out in a school corridor.

Thankfully, based on my knowledge of the layout of this

place, it doesn't take me long to make it to where I'm going. The receptionist behind her desk looks and acts like the overworked and underpaid gatekeeper that she is, appearing tired and already bored but willing to make things difficult for anybody who hasn't made an appointment to be here.

I recognise her from the last time I was here, which must have been about eighteen months ago, when Jacob got a detention, although it turned out to be a case of mistaken identity. His History teacher, Mr Jenkins, had got Jacob mixed up with another pupil in his class who he thought was talking during the lesson, and he'd handed out the punishment to the wrong person. But after Jacob told me his pleas of innocence had fallen on deaf ears, I had come to the school to right the issue myself. I know it makes me seem like one of those awful mothers who thinks her child can do no wrong and protests at every detention they might get, as if they are innocent little angels who never commit a sin, but, in that case, Jacob actually was innocent so of course I was going to protect him.

Just like I'm going to protect him now, although, as of yet, I don't know exactly what it is I'm protecting him from.

'I'd like to speak to Mrs Vigon, please,' I say after taking a deep breath to calm down. It's never good to appear in front of a headmistress in an angry or distracted state, and I learnt that lesson the hard way from my own school days many years ago. Unlike my son, all the detentions I got were entirely warranted.

I have to spend five minutes convincing the receptionist that my presence here is warranted and that, while I am happy to wait, I won't leave until my concerns have been heard. Eventually, after flicking through a very dry education magazine in which the future of teaching is predicted to be dominated by AI technology in a hundred years' time, something I find startling and amusing in equal measure, I am shown through to the office of Mrs Vigon, the woman with all the power in this place.

'Thanks for seeing me,' I say as I take a seat.

'You're Jacob's mother?' Mrs Vigon asks, clearly having been prepped by her receptionist before I entered.

'Yes, that's right.'

'You came to see me last year if I remember correctly. Something about a detention.'

'Err, yes, but this is about something else now.'

'Is everything okay?'

'I hope so, but I'm not sure. I'm worried that my son might be being bullied.'

I'm unsure what impact the 'B' word will have on a headmistress who has surely seen and heard it all during her time in professional education. However, it does land with the gravity intended because her expression turns serious, and she pauses to gather her thoughts before speaking again.

'Oh, I'm terribly sorry to hear that. What has happened?'

'That's the problem. I don't know because Jacob won't tell me.'

'So how do you know he's being bullied?'

'I just do. He's acting odd. Faking illness. Not wanting to go to school. He's never been like this before. And my husband heard him crying in the middle of the night.'

'Oh, that's awful, and I'm sorry to hear that, but as far as I'm aware, he hasn't had any problems here.'

'Something must be going on to have him so worked up like this. He tried to run out of my car on the way here this morning.'

'Again, I'm sorry, but I don't know what you want me to say. If he makes an allegation against another pupil, then we will take it very seriously and investigate thoroughly, but until then, there's not much I can do.'

'Not much you can do? Is that what you would have said to Zoe Atkinson's parents when she was being bullied? Or would you have saved that gem of wisdom until after she had killed herself?'

I know I shouldn't have said that almost as soon as the words leave my mouth because – one, it's outrageous, and two, Zoe attended a different school to this one, so whatever mistakes were made in authority, no blame can be laid at Mrs Vigon's door.

'I'm sorry,' I say before taking a deep breath. 'I'm just worried about my son.'

'And I can appreciate that,' Mrs Vigon replies, showing some class on her part after my rather unclassy showing. 'If it helps, I can ask some of the teachers to keep an eye on Jacob and let me know if they see anything untoward going on with him.'

'I'd appreciate that, thank you.'

'Apart from that, maybe just keep trying to talk to your son. I'm sure if something is troubling him, then he will tell you eventually. If not, maybe it's nothing. Just typical teenage things. Lord knows we have enough of those types of problems here on a daily basis.'

I nod my head and thank Mrs Vigon for her time, figuring I've said everything I came here to say, as well as a whole lot more that I shouldn't have. I also have to put a little trust in her vast experience in overseeing a building full of youngsters and, for the most part, there are never any serious issues arising from that, so she must be doing a good enough job on the whole.

But then again, it only takes one slip-up for things to totally fall apart.

As I leave the school and get back into my car, I glance back at the big building with the rows of windows and wonder which classroom my son will be in now. Wherever he is, I just hope he is okay.

Is he?

I guess only time will tell on that front.

EIGHT

GUY

It's Saturday and that usually means one thing: a big lie-in to celebrate the first day this week when I don't have to haul my tired bones out of bed and rush to work in a race against the clock. But while I usually sleep in until at least nine on the weekends now the kids are older, today is different. That's because Sara is awake, and when she's awake, everybody else in the house is awake too.

'What are you doing?' I ask her as she walks in and out of the bedroom several times, seemingly ignoring the fact that the curtains are still closed and I'm trying to doze.

'Just getting on with the housework,' she says before picking up the laundry basket and disappearing again. But after hearing the washing machine go on downstairs, she's back a moment later, this time with a charity bag, and she wastes no time opening her wardrobe and pulling out some old garments to put in the bag.

'Look, it's great that you're doing your bit for charity, but do you really have to do it now, at eight fifteen?' I say wearily, my head still buried in my pillow but my eyes open and sleep a distant dream now.

'No time like the present,' Sara replies as she continues to bundle her unwanted clothes into the bag.

I consider having another go at getting her to relax and let the day grow a little bit older before she carries on making so much noise, but I know it's futile because I know exactly why she's up early and keeping herself so busy. It's because she's still worried about Jacob, and when Sara is worried, she goes into overdrive.

This is similar to the time when we were waiting for some test results back from the hospital, after a slight health scare with Amber when she was six. Sara spent the week that we were waiting to hear back from the specialist scrubbing every inch of this house to the point where I had to prise the bottles of bleach out of her hand and tell her to sit down for a moment. I get that people deal with stressful situations in their own way, and Sara's way is to do house chores, which is a lot healthier than other distraction methods, I suppose, but it's still all a symptom of her being anxious, and that is not healthy.

But what can I say to get her to stop? Jacob is still acting strange, his day at school yesterday not seeming to do anything to improve his mood, and once again he went to bed very early last night without saying much and eating very little. As long as that's the case, Sara will worry about him, as will I. But I can't bear the thought of spending the whole day in this house with a tormented teen in his bedroom and a frazzled wife constantly tidying up under my feet, so I rack my brains to come up with a plan that might improve all our moods.

'Rovers are playing at home today. How about I try and get tickets and take Jacob?' I suggest before Sara can turn her attention to my wardrobe and start throwing some of my old clothes out as well.

'You think he'll want to go?'

'It's his favourite football team. If that doesn't cheer him up, I don't know what will.'

Thankfully, Sara is quickly on board, so I leave her to the charity bags and quickly get changed, pulling on my replica Rovers jersey before venturing into Jacob's room to let him know my plan.

I find my son sat up on his bed playing a video game on low volume, but that's far better than hearing him crying like I did the other day, so I take a seat beside him and ask him how he's getting on with the game.

'All right,' he mumbles back, before his character dies and he has to start the level again.

'Me. You. A Rovers match. And a bag of chips on the way home. What do you say?' I suggest, tapping the club badge on my jersey to emphasise my point.

I expect the same reaction such a suggestion has always got over the years, and that is Jacob smiling widely before quickly rushing to put on his own jersey and then asking me if we can get some food before the match too. But that doesn't happen this time. Jacob is keen because he nods his head and says okay, but there is none of the excitement he usually displays. It's better than nothing, and I tell him we'll leave in the next hour so we can have a leisurely walk to the stadium before the midday kick-off.

I spend the rest of the morning helping Sara with the 'spring clean', even though it's early autumn – hoovering, dusting and taking out the bin bags, and by the time Jacob joins us downstairs with his shirt and jacket on, I can't wait to get going.

'Enjoy the match!' Sara calls to us as we leave, and I make a joke about how we'll only enjoy it if our team does a better job of defending than they did in last week's game, before I pull the door closed behind us.

. . .

'Nice day for it,' I say as Jacob and I begin our thirty-minute walk to the ground, a route that takes us through the town and along the river, which is actually quite pleasant on the rare days it isn't raining.

Jacob is not as chatty as usual, but I don't allow any awkwardness to build between us, making sure I keep engaging with him, mostly talking about fun things that I'm sure he'll be receptive to, like who the manager might play in attack today and whether or not I can put a sneaky bet on the final result without his mum finding out.

To further improve my son's mood, I buy him a cheese-burger from one of the vendors outside the ground, and his appetite seems to have returned as he hungrily wolfs it down, making me even more convinced that getting him out of the house was the right thing to do. But whatever has been trou-bling him is still a secret, so I plan to try and coax it out of him a little later on. First, we have a game to watch, and I'm hoping it's a good game because, if so, that will only cheer my son up even more and increase the chances of him finally letting me in on what's been on his mind in the last few days.

We join the ten thousand or so other people inside the stadium just in time to see the referee start proceedings, and the first half whizzes by in a flurry of missed chances, bad tackles and some questionable officiating. At halftime it's o–o: not the most exciting scoreline, but Jacob seems to be enjoying himself and has been a little chattier since we got here, although it's all been football talk so far.

Just before the second half kicks off, my son removes his jacket, clearly having got a little too warm on this unseasonable autumn day, and when he does, I notice his football jersey rise up a little on his torso before he can get it back into position.

And that's when I see the bruises along the right side of his ribcage.

Jacob has no idea that I've noticed them, and I pretend to be focused on the match more than him, but now that I've seen those injuries, I can't stop thinking about them.

How did he get them? Who has hurt him?

Is this why he has been acting strange these last few days?

I'm facing the pitch and watching the players run around on it, but I'm barely paying attention to any of the action, and before I know it, the referee calls full-time. We've lost 0–1, which is a poor result, but I couldn't care less about league tables or the consequences of the manager's tactics now. All I want to know is how my son got those bruises, and I'll only find that out if he tells me.

Years of parenting have taught me that if you want your children to do something, you often have to sweeten them up first, so with that in mind, I lead Jacob away from the stadium and into a fish and chip shop, where we quickly give our order before taking a seat at one of the small tables. It's here, sitting on these blue plastic chairs with a big bottle of vinegar and a huge tub of salt in between us, that I tentatively broach the difficult subject with Jacob.

'How did you get those bruises?' I ask him as he tucks into his chips, though he stops eating as soon as I've spoken.

'What?'

'I saw them at the game when you took your jacket off. How did you get them?'

Jacob looks very pale and very worried.

'You're not in any trouble,' I assure him. 'I just want to know what happened.'

Jacob is still reluctant.

'Look, if you tell me, then we can talk about it and maybe, just maybe, I won't have to tell your mum, if you don't want me to. But if you don't tell me, then I'll have no choice, and believe me, she will not let you out of the house ever again until you tell her what's going on.'

I don't need to convince Jacob that what I've just said is true because he knows it as well as I do, and that seems to be the thing that gets him talking.

'I got into a fight,' he admits with a shrug. 'That's all.'

'A fight? Who with?'

'Nobody.'

'Jacob?'

'Just a guy at school. It was during a football match at lunchtime.'

'What happened? How did it start?'

'He did a bad tackle on James,' he says, referring to his best mate.

'And?'

'I pushed him off James. He pushed me back, and I fell over. Then he kicked me a couple of times in the ribs.'

'He kicked you in the ribs! He can't do that!'

'It's fine.'

'No, it's not. Did you tell any of the teachers?'

'No, no way. I'm not doing that.'

'You have to! He can't behave like that! Pushing is one thing but kicking you when you're on the ground – that's extremely dangerous.'

I'm furious that some kid thinks it's okay to kick anyone when they're down, never mind my own son. If only it wasn't a Saturday, then I'd drive over to the school right now and demand to speak to somebody.

'Dad, just leave it, please. It's fine.'

'No, it's not fine. Let me have another look at those bruises. Are you in pain?'

'Dad, just leave it!'

Jacob abandons his chips then and leaves the table, running out the door of the chip shop, and I have to rush after him. I catch him up on the street just around the corner from where we were eating and, when I do, I tell him he can't let the boy get away with what he's done. But that only seems to make Jacob more frustrated.

'No, just leave it!'

'Why?'

'Because he'll do it again if I say anything!'

'What?'

Jacob tries to walk away then, but I grab his hand and, as he keeps pulling, I notice tears running down his cheeks.

'Hey, buddy. Come here. It's okay,' I say as I attempt to pull him in for a hug, and despite resisting for another few seconds, he eventually concedes. When he does, it's as if the floodgates open, and he sobs into my chest in a way he hasn't done since he was a very small child after he'd hurt himself on something.

I say nothing, just stroking his hair and waiting for him to calm down, and he eventually does, wiping his eyes with the sleeve of his jacket and apologising for getting the front of my jersey all wet. I don't care about that, I just want him to be okay, but based on what I've seen and heard here today, I don't think that he is.

The fight. The bruises. The fear. It sounds like he is afraid of something like this happening again.

'Tell me the boy's name,' I say. 'And I'll make sure it doesn't happen again.'

'No,' Jacob replies, shaking his head. 'Can we just go home now?'

'You have to tell me.'

'No, I don't.'

I get the sense that Jacob is going to run again and I don't want that, because while I caught up to him this time, I might not do so again, and I don't want him out here all day and night without me knowing where he is. That's why I agree to drop it for the time being and suggest we make our way back home.

Jacob says he plans to spend the rest of the day playing his video games, and I don't argue with him, even though I know that's not what is going to happen at all.

Not when I tell his mother about those bruises.

NINE

SARA

'How was the match?' I ask as my two favourite males walk through the door, the pair of them giving off the distinctive smell that I always associate with men going to the football, which is mainly fried food and second-hand cigarette smoke.

'It was all right,' Jacob says before he heads for the stairs, and when I go to stop him so I can talk to him more, Guy gestures to tell me to let him go.

I do as he wishes, and once Jacob is in his room, I ask Guy what is going on.

'Let's have a cup of tea first,' he suggests, but that just makes me suspicious, as if he's trying to get me to relax before he gives me some bad news. I'd rather just hear it, whatever it is, so I push him on it until he finally spills. When he does, he tells me about the bruises he saw on Jacob's body before enlightening me about how he got them.

'What?' I cry, guessing my facial expression is a mixture of anguish and anger. But, of course, it is because I'm shocked and upset by the news. Somebody beat up my son during a game of football at school?

Guy admits that it is a bad thing, but then tries to suggest that it's a positive thing that Jacob admitted what happened to him in the end, because it shows he's not completely shutting us out. But I'm going to need far more than that, and after Guy says he still doesn't know the name of the boy who kicked Jacob in the ribs, I head up the staircase to get some answers up there.

'Just wait a minute,' Guy says, clearly afraid of a raging argument erupting. 'If you push him, then he might clam up and never tell us.'

I ignore his concerns and enter Jacob's bedroom, interrupting my son and his video game, and I don't even give him a chance to speak before I hit the power button and turn the television off.

'Hey!' Jacob cries, the console controller still in his hands though the game has stopped.

'Let me see those bruises,' I say, and I try to get Jacob to lift his jersey, but he wriggles away from me.

'Get off me!' he cries before looking at Guy, and I can see he is angry at him for telling me. But what was Guy supposed to do?

'Your mum's just worried about you, as am I,' Guy says. 'We just want to make sure you're okay and that this won't happen again.'

'It won't.'

'How do you know that for sure?' I ask, and I study our son for any more injuries, even though none are visibly on show.

'Please, just leave me alone,' Jacob begs, but I can see he's on the verge of tears, which does nothing to fill me with any confidence that he genuinely thinks this issue is over.

'If he's bullying you, then you have to tell us,' I say. 'Just give us his name, and we can talk to the school. They'll make it stop.'

Jacob shakes his head as his eyes continue to water.

'Jacob! This is serious! Look what happened to Zoe!'

'I'm not going to kill myself!'

'That's probably what her parents thought too, right before she did it!'

Guy tries to get me to calm down, but I'm too fired up now, and can he blame me? Nobody wants a repeat of what happened to poor Zoe. Bullies are the lowest of the low and need to be stopped before they do any more damage. But how can we get our son to tell us the boy's name if he doesn't want to?

'I'll ask James,' I say, remembering that Guy told me that Jacob said his best friend was present during the football match when the injuries to his ribs were sustained.

'What?'

'I'll ask James if you don't tell us. I'll go over to his house now and speak to his parents. Tell them how worried I am. They'll get their son to talk. I'll go right now if you don't tell me.'

I mean it, and I turn to the door, genuinely ready to get in the car and drive to my son's friend's place. But Jacob stops me and, when he does, he seems to realise that he can't keep this a secret forever.

'It's Mason,' he says quietly, his head bowed and his eyes closed.

'What?' I say because I barely heard him, but Guy seems to have got it.

'Mason Burton? The boy who bullied Zoe?'

Jacob nods his head and stifles a sob.

'You've got to be kidding me,' I cry, incredulous. 'That boy is bullying someone else now? What, one child taking her life wasn't enough for him? He wants the same thing to happen to somebody else?'

I can feel the anger rising up inside me, and I imagine Guy is feeling the same way. My fists are clenched, and my heart is pounding, and at this precise moment in time all I can think of is getting my hands on that despicable human being who hurt Zoe and is now hurting my son.

'Just leave it. Don't do anything or it'll be worse for me,' Jacob tells us, so serious I can see the fear on his face; but he can't honestly expect us not to do anything with this news.

Guy storms out of the room then, evidently on the warpath, and I go after him once I've checked that Jacob is okay. He's not, and he pleads with me again not to do anything, but I tell him to just stay in his room, and we'll talk later, which is ironic considering how long I've spent trying to get him to come out of his room these past few days.

I find Guy in the kitchen pacing around with his phone in his hand.

'What are you doing?' I ask him.

'I'm thinking about calling the police and reporting that boy!' he cries, and I can see he means it.

'Wait! This is a matter for the school, not the police.'

'Is it? The last time that boy bullied somebody, they ended up dead. I think the police should hear about this!'

'Just calm down and let's talk about this.'

'What is there to talk about? Somebody kicked our son in the ribs when he was on the ground, several times, and now we know it's Mason! And we know all about him, don't we? Everybody in this town does!'

'Which is why we have to be careful.'

'What?'

'You can see how worried Jacob is. He doesn't want to get in trouble for snitching.'

'I don't give a damn about that. That boy wants locking up. He should have been behind bars years ago, and they should have thrown away the key!'

'I agree with you completely, you know I do, but the fact is he's still a minor, so the police won't do anything anyway. We need to talk to the school.'

'But it's the weekend.'

'Then we go in on Monday.'

'I don't want to wait until then.'

'Neither do I, but what else can we do?'

I seem to have persuaded Guy to hold off on calling the police, and after he puts the phone down, I have him take a seat with me at the table.

'I could kill that boy,' I say, scaring myself a little because I actually mean it.

'Me too,' Guy repeats, and that's just as scary because I know he means it too. I don't want to waste all my energy thinking about somebody who doesn't deserve it, so I turn my thoughts back to my poor son upstairs.

'Should we take him to the hospital? They might need to look at his ribs.'

'I don't know. I guess. He doesn't seem like he's in much pain, though. I'm guessing there's no break or fracture, or we'd have found out about it a lot sooner.'

'Oh, I guess we're lucky then. Our son only got badly beaten, but it's fine because there are no broken bones.'

'I didn't mean it like that.'

'I know, I'm sorry,' I say, trying to calm down again but it feels impossible to do so. I'd have been furious about whoever had done this to Jacob, never mind the circumstances. But finding out that it's Mason, that boy with a horrible history? *That just makes me feel sick.*

'What if we hadn't found out about this?' I say, tears filling my eyes now. 'What if he'd managed to keep it secret like Zoe did? What if he'd hurt himself?'

'Hey, don't think like that. This is different. Jacob wouldn't do that.'

'How do you know? He was crying himself to sleep the

other night. How do we know what he's thinking? You saw how he didn't want to go to school yesterday. The poor boy's terrified.'

Guy can't argue with that, but he just reassures me again that Jacob will be fine. But the anger is still etched all over his face, and we both lament the fact that it's Saturday afternoon, and we can't speak to the school for at least another thirty-six hours. Until then, the priority is making sure Jacob is okay, so I tell Guy that I'm going to go and check on him, and I won't leave his room until he has let me have a proper look at his bruises. I want to see them for myself and, for all I know, Guy could be downplaying the severity of them, either to save his son's embarrassment or because he wants to save himself from spending Saturday night sitting in A & E with him. It wouldn't be the first time my husband has adopted a 'let's wait and see' approach when it comes to any injuries our children might have picked up over the years. He'd much rather that than spend four hours waiting to see a doctor or nurse who will most likely tell him it was fine after all. But isn't it always better to be safe than sorry?

As I head for the stairs, Guy tells me he will be up soon to help me have another go at checking Jacob's bruises, and as I leave the kitchen, I expect he will be right behind me. But he's not.

He's taking a whiskey glass out of the cupboard, and now he's looking for the bottle that goes with it.

I guess that's how he plans to get through the rest of this weekend.

Typical.

TEN

GUY

It's ten o'clock on a Saturday night, and not for the first time in my life, I've had too much to drink. I know there are never any answers to be found at the bottom of a bottle, but that's never stopped me from searching, and that's why I've been sipping whiskey ever since Jacob told me who gave him those injuries.

I'd feel like wringing the neck of anybody who harmed my son, but hearing that it was Mason, a low-life thug who has already caused enough pain to other people in this town, was almost too much to bear. I wanted to do something, anything, to stop myself from sitting around the house and feeling useless, but with it being the weekend, Sara was quite right in saying we'd have to wait until Monday before we could go to the school. At a loose end, then, I've turned to drink, and once Jacob assured us that his injuries did not require the attention of a medical professional, I've been sitting on the sofa ever since, getting progressively inebriated and trying to take Sara's advice to calm down and think about something else.

It's easier said than done, and she knows it as well as I do. She can try and pretend all she wants like she's not thinking about Mason, but I know her mind is racing just as much as mine is. I guess she's just better at dealing with it than I am, and the strongest thing she's been sipping on so far today is tea. But I'm not my wife, and I have my own way of dealing with things, even if that way usually ends up resulting in a hangover the following day.

'How much have you had?' Sara asks me when she sees me reaching for the bottle again.

'It's Saturday night,' I say with a shrug, but she'll know that's no excuse, just as I do.

I pretend to be concentrating on the film Sara selected and started an hour ago, but, if I'm honest, I've got absolutely no idea what's going on or who any of the characters are. I couldn't care less about this movie and whatever crazy plot it might have, because as far as I'm concerned, there is more than enough drama going on in the real world right now.

'Are you even watching this?' Sara asks me, reading me like a book, and while I pretend that I am, a couple of quick questions from her about who is who in this film gives away my position.

'Right, that's it! We're going to bed,' she says, suddenly turning off the TV with the remote.

'Hey, it's still early,' I say, yet another generous measure of whiskey in my hand.

'Neither of us is watching this and I know why. Let's just get this day over with, and we'll feel a bit better about things after a good night's sleep.'

Sara might be being sensible, but I'm in no mood to agree with the voice of reason, not when I've got half a bottle of something strong inside me. That's why I dispute her idea of going upstairs; instead I grab the remote and turn the TV back on so I can continue watching it alone.

I'm actually glad when Sara leaves me to it because I'm not seeking company at the present time. I just want to stew by myself; nothing but me, this bottle and my dark thoughts about what I would do to Mason if I ever got my hands on him.

I'm aware that an adult doing anything violent to a fifteen year old would be unsavoury, but try telling me that Kevin Atkinson has not been daydreaming about doing even worse things to that schoolboy. After what happened to his daughter, I'd be amazed if Kevin hasn't come up with a million ingenious ways that he could get his own back on Mason, and I'm sure many of them involve sharp objects. But as far as I'm aware, Kevin restrained from inflicting any physical violence on his child's bully, so if he can do it, surely I can do it too. That's why I decide to make this drink my last one before going upstairs to join my wife in bed.

But it's as I'm passing Jacob's room that I see the light still on underneath his door. Figuring he's still awake, I poke my head in and see him lying in his bed reading a book. But, of course, he's lying on his left side because his right must still be too tender to put any weight on it.

'Hey, buddy. How's it going?' I whisper, keeping my voice low so Sara won't hear me and come out to see what's going on, because I want this private moment with my son.

Jacob lowers his book and smiles at me, but when he does, I see he has been crying again.

'I'm okay,' he lies. 'Just tired.'

'Try and get some sleep,' I tell him, and he puts his book down before reaching for the lamp beside his bed.

'Night, Dad,' he says. 'Thanks for taking me to the match.'

'You're welcome, buddy. Just a shame about the result.'

We share a smile before the light goes off, and I leave the room, satisfied that my son is not mad at me any more after telling his mum what he told me in the chip shop. But that's about all I'm satisfied with, because seeing that Jacob had been crying again, as well as knowing that he is forced to only sleep on his left side because of the bruising on his right, makes my blood start to boil again, and despite planning on going to my bedroom, I instead find myself going back downstairs.

I quietly put my shoes on and grab my jacket before leaving the house and setting off down the street, walking briskly in the cool night air, warmed by the whiskey and emboldened by its potency. I walk for almost twenty minutes until I reach my destination.

Harper Close, a street in the rougher part of town.

Glancing left and right to see the numbers on the front doors, I eventually make my way to Number 47, and when I get there, I stop because I recognise this house. I've seen it on the news. This is where several journalists gathered to try and interview the occupants back when they were at the heart of the biggest story to ever grip this town. The journalists didn't have much success in getting their soundbites, but they did record plenty of footage that was broadcast on the news, including footage of the homeowners going in and out of the house while trying to evade the media.

This is where Mason lives with his parents.

Having read enough news articles about them, I could remember their address off by heart, and I know they still live here because I recognise the licence plate of the van on the drive.

THE BO55

Mason's father, Dean, owns this vehicle, and I know that because I saw it on the news too. I also learnt from an article that Dean runs his own plumbing company, hence him calling himself 'The Boss'. It's a tacky, gaudy thing to have on a licence plate, but, of course, it suits this family down to the ground, and it's no surprise that Mason is an arrogant little so-and-so because his father clearly is.

I march past the van and towards the front door, noting that there is a light on downstairs, so I'm guessing the family is still up. It wouldn't make much difference if they were in bed, though, because I'd still make sure to knock loud enough for them to hear me, and as I begin pounding on the door, I suspect I'm going to wake a few neighbours up too. Although I don't care about that, and as I keep banging on the door with my fists, I see movement through the frosted glass that tells me somebody is coming to see what all the noise is about.

Hiccupping slightly and tasting a little whiskey in my mouth as I stop knocking, I'm aware that my being here tonight is fuelled by my excessive alcohol consumption earlier. It's too late to have second thoughts now because the door is unlocked, and I'm face to face with 'the boss' himself – one of the two people responsible for creating that terror of a child.

Dean Burton.

'Who the hell are you? Do you know what time it is?' Dean says to me, his narrow eyes glaring at me and his lips curled into a snarl. That's not all I notice about his appearance. I can see a few tufts of his chest hair poking out from beneath the dressing gown that is loosely fastened across his torso, as well as the fact he is barefoot. He looks like he wasn't far off going to bed. But before he can do that, he'll have to deal with me.

'Are you Mason Burton's father?' I ask, even though I already know the answer.

'Who's asking?' comes the defiant response.

'I'm the father of Jacob Holdsworth, the boy who has a set of severely bruised ribs after your son kicked him several times during a football match at school,' I say back, forgoing any subtlety or acts of politeness because this man in front of me is not making any effort on those grounds either.

I wonder if that statement will get this man to be a little

more understanding about my reasons for being here so late at night, but it doesn't seem to do the trick.

'What's that got to do with me?'

'Well, your son attacked my son. I don't think that's right, do you?'

'Oh, piss off.'

Dean tries to shut his door then, but I shoot out an arm to prevent the door from being closed, and Dean does not like that. But it's too bad because I've not finished talking yet.

'Not only that but Mason has threatened my son into not telling anybody about what happened, and by the sounds of it, he's been nothing but a bully. Given your son's history with bullying, I thought you should know, and now I want to know what you're going to do about it.'

'You've got five seconds to get away from this door, or I'll show you what I'm going to do about it,' Dean snarls, and it's clear the apple doesn't fall far from the tree in this family. This man is as big a bully as his son.

'Dad, what's going on?'

The young voice behind Dean in the hallway causes the homeowner to turn around, and when he does, I see Mason standing on the staircase. He's much bigger than the last time I saw him, which would have been in the school playground after he had begun attending the same place where I dropped my son off. He's certainly much bigger than how I remember him in all those photos in the local newspaper, back when the reports of Zoe's death due to bullying were first circulating and shocking the residents of this town. But even with the passage of time, I'd recognise that expression of his anywhere.

He's even more smug than his father is.

'There you are, you little scumbag. You keep your hands off my son, do you hear me?' I cry, launching into a tirade against the youngster lurking in the hallway. 'I know what you did to him, and if you so much as touch him again, then

I'll have the police around here to arrest you, do you hear me?'

I feel vindicated in what I'm saying, but in my anger, I've failed to notice that Dean is suddenly lunging towards me.

Feeling his strong hands on my chest, he pushes me away from his door, and I stumble backwards, only just about maintaining my balance, which is a miracle considering how hard I was pushed and how much whiskey I've had tonight. Not to be deterred, I move back towards the door, and despite Dean warning me to get lost, I have no intention of heeding that order.

Instead, I just clench my right fist tightly before launching it in Dean's direction.

Making a connection with the side of his face, I hear the man groan, and now it's his turn to stagger backwards. I feel as though I've just done as much damage to my hand as I've done to him, and as I look at my hand to inspect it I see blood across the knuckles.

And that's when I realise I'm in very big trouble.

ELEVEN

SARA

I woke up with a fright to the sound of the house phone ringing, and when I answered it, I got just as big a shock.

'Hello? Is that Mrs Holdsworth?'

'Yes, who's this?'

'This is PC Straw calling from Anderton Station. I'm just calling to let you know that we have your husband here in custody.'

'What?'

Absolutely none of what I just heard made any sense, and I grip the receiver tightly, praying that I've still not quite woken up yet and that this is just part of a bad dream. But it's not. I'm fully awake, but if anything, things just get even worse.

'He was involved in an altercation, and the other party has expressed their wish to press charges.'

'What are you talking about? What's happened?'

'If you could come down to the station, you'll be able to speak to your husband here.'

I feel like I'm in a daze as I put down the phone and start getting dressed, replacing my pyjamas with more suitable clothing as I prepare to go outside in the middle of the night. I do remember glancing at the clock and seeing that it is half past two in the morning, which explains my sleepy, confused state. What it does not explain is why my husband is in a police station instead of lying next to me in bed.

I knew he hadn't come upstairs by midnight but figured he was still sat in the living room drinking whiskey and watching TV. I guess I'd fallen asleep not long after that and expected to wake up in the morning with Guy next to me, no doubt with a sore head and a stinking hangover but at least where he belongs. Now I find out that he's been involved in some kind of an altercation, and charges are being pressed...

What on earth has happened?

'Mum, what's going on?'

Jacob catches me off guard, and I spin around to the bedroom doorway to see my son in his pyjamas, rubbing his eyes.

'Nothing. Go back to bed.'

'I heard the phone.'

I'm not sure what to say, but I can't think that telling Jacob what is going on with his father is a wise move at this time of night. Better for our son to handle whatever it may be in the morning, and I certainly don't want to be dragging him out to the police station. Me having to go is bad enough.

'It was your father. He's out, but I'm just going to get him.'

'Out? Where is he?'

'He went to meet a friend.'

'Who?'

'It doesn't matter. Go back to bed. I'll lock the front door, and we'll be back soon.'

It's a relief when Jacob does as he is told, but I guess he didn't need too much persuading to return to his warm, comfy bed. I sure wish I could crawl back into mine as well, but as it is, I'm putting my shoes and coat on, and now I'm starting the car, desperately waiting for some warm air to come out of the heaters so my hands won't be so cold as I make my drive across town.

It's a good thing the roads are empty at this time of night because my mind is all over the place as I try and figure out what all this is about while battling fatigue and a general sense of unease. I'm still none the wiser as I park at the station beside several police cars, and as I rush inside, I am desperate for answers.

After giving my name to a male police officer behind a Perspex screen, I sit anxiously on a plastic chair in what I guess is a waiting room of sorts, until another police officer comes and speaks to me. When they do, I am greeted by PC Straw, the woman I spoke to on the phone earlier, and she invites me into a small room where we can talk in private.

'Please tell me what is going on?' I say as I take a seat opposite PC Straw at a small table. 'Is my husband okay?'

'Your husband is fine.'

'Where is he?'

'He's currently in a holding room while we wait for him to sober up.'

'Sober up? Oh my god, what has he done?'

'Like I said on the phone, he was involved in an altercation.'

'He got into a fight?'

'It would seem that way, yes.'

'Who with?'

'We're still gathering all the details at the moment.'

'You must know who it was with! Are they here? Have you arrested them too?'

'An officer is speaking to them at the moment, yes.'

'Why can't you tell me who they are?'

'I just wanted to let you know what was going on with your partner so that you weren't worrying.'

'But I'm still worrying because I don't know what's going on! Is he in trouble?'

'We need to get all the facts, but, like I said, we won't be doing that until the morning when your husband has had time to sober up and calm down.'

'Sober up and calm down?'

I think back to the last time I saw Guy. I left him in the living room as I went up to bed. He had a big glass of whiskey with him, though it was far from his first. What happened between then and now? How much more did he drink? And what on earth did he do to end up in here?

I keep asking more questions, but PC Straw tells me I will be able to speak to my husband in a few hours, once he has been questioned and assuming they are happy to release him. But I don't like that it comes down to an assumption rather than hard fact, so I spend the next couple of hours stressing out in the waiting room before I feel like it's a more suitable hour to call my friend, Shirley, and wake her up. Then I ask her if she wouldn't mind going to my house soon and checking that Jacob is okay, telling her where the spare key is hidden in the back garden and just giving some vague story about me and Jacob's father being called away on unexpected business.

Shirley agrees to help me out, so with Jacob taken care of when he wakes up soon, I can focus on my husband now and getting him out of whatever mess he has got himself into.

Another ninety minutes pass by before I get my first glimpse of Guy and, when I do, I'm shocked to see his face. That's because he's sporting a sizeable injury, a dark circle of bruising around his left eye that tells me he must have been punched by somebody. Just as shocking to me is seeing him in handcuffs. As he's marched past me, I leap out of my seat and try to get to him.

'Guy! Are you okay? What's going on?' I ask, but the two police officers accompanying him make sure I keep my distance, telling me they are taking him to be questioned and that I'll be able to speak to him soon.

'I'm okay,' Guy tells me, though he looks very sheepish as he is led away, not at all like the bright, energetic man I know so well.

I can't sit down again after that and end up pacing around in the waiting room for the best part of the next hour, all the while fearing that Guy has done something terrible when he was drunk and that our lives are never going to be the same again. It wouldn't be the first time I've been concerned about Guy's alcohol intake, and I have passed comment on it before, though it has been difficult to get him to listen too much as it's how he chooses to unwind, and I can't fault him for being a hard worker. But I've often worried he might take it too far one day, either from a health standpoint or by doing something stupid after one too many drinks. Now it seems the latter worry has come true.

I just wish I knew what had happened and who he had been fighting with.

And then I get a clue.

I recognise the man passing by the waiting room with a police officer leading the way. It's Dean Burton, the father of Mason Burton. I'd recognise that pig-ugly face of his anywhere, or maybe that's just because I saw him sneering once when a microphone and camera were shoved in his face, and he was asked if he regretted what his son had done with regards to causing Zoe's suicide. The fact he hadn't said yes or offered any sympathy or condolences at the time spoke volumes about his character, and I remember my blood turning cold when I saw him on TV that day all those years ago. My blood has turned even colder now I've just seen him again, because putting two and two together, I can figure out why my husband is under arrest, especially when I see that Dean is sporting a black eye too.

Guy must have attacked Dean over what his son did to Jacob.

I guess he was defending his honour or simply trying to get Mason's dad to control his son a little better.

But people can't be going around throwing punches and expect to get away with it, can they?

So what is going to happen to my husband now?

TWELVE

GUY

I've never experienced a headache as bad as this one, not even in my student days, when I used to stay up all night, drinking copious amounts of cheap liquor, before turning up for 9 a.m. classes beneath the bright lights of an enormous lecture hall. Then again, I did drink a hell of a lot last night, or maybe it's because I got punched in the face too.

I guess that can't have helped, can it?

Whether it was a hangover or a mild concussion that was making my head throb, I could have seriously done without it, sitting across a table from a police officer who wanted to question me about my actions at the Burton household last night.

It was no fun to have to face up to the consequences of my actions, however justified I felt they might have been and, as the police officer made it clear, I'm now in big trouble unless Dean Burton drops the charges, which I'm not confident he will. His face is just as bruised as mine, so I don't think he'll be doing me any favours anytime soon.

Despite explaining to the police officer why I went to the house and got so angry, it did little to change the facts. The police officer expressed some sympathy when I told him what had happened to Jacob, but quite sensibly, and I'm sure quite rightly, he told me that members of the public couldn't just go around taking matters into their own hands. If there was a problem with bullying or anything like that, then it was either a matter for the school or the police to deal with, not Joe Public and certainly not a drunken, angry Joe Public.

In the end, I realised I wasn't getting anywhere by trying to defend myself, so I stopped talking and accepted what I was told. I've now been released on bail, though I am facing charges of assault, not to mention trespassing, harassment and one count of 'Disturbing the Peace'. All of that adds up to the potential for a jail term or, at best, a fine and community service, none of which is appealing and all of which makes me feel ashamed, as well as super-stressed. It didn't make a difference to my defence when I said Dean pushed me away from his door, because, as the homeowner, the police say he had a right to if he felt threatened, which, of course, he has told them he did. All they care about is who threw the first punch and, unfortunately for me, I did.

Damn Dean for pressing charges against me. The thought of having to stand up in a courtroom and face the wrath of the law is a daunting one. How does a person prepare for that? On top of that, I'm sure my employer will have something to say about it all when they find out this week. It can't be good to have an employee who's in trouble with the police, and maybe I should check my contract to see what the HR policy is on that. But at the moment, I'm not worried about facing a judge, a jury or my boss quite yet. That's because I've got to face my wife first, and I can't expect she is going to take too kindly to what I've done either.

Her reaction to this will most likely blow all the others out of the water.

I find her in the same waiting room I briefly saw her in before I was questioned, but at least this time the handcuffs have been removed from my wrists, and I look like less of a criminal. Okay, so I still look like a hungover fool who's been in a fight of my own making, but it could be worse.

'Please tell me what's happened,' Sara says, and I feel bad for the fact she's had to be waiting in here all this time while I've been sorting out my problems elsewhere, so I promise to tell her once we're out of the station, and as soon as we're in the car, I keep my word.

I enlighten her on my ill-fated walk to the Burton home and all the drama that ensued when I got there.

'Are you stupid? What the hell were you thinking?' she cries, taking it about as well as I could have hoped.

'I know I shouldn't have gone there, but I was just so angry.'

'You think that gives you an excuse to run around town punching people?'

'I wasn't randomly punching people. I punched Dean, and, trust me, you would have wanted to punch him as well if you were there too. You should have seen the guy. It was as if he didn't care at all what his son did to other people. You'd think he'd have been mortified after what happened with Zoe, but he didn't give a damn. I can certainly see where Mason gets it from, not that it's any excuse.'

I'm hoping Sara might calm down a little bit after hearing how bad Dean was when I confronted him, but she doesn't.

'Do you have any idea what it felt like to be woken up in the middle of the night with a phone call from the police? I was worried sick. Anything could have happened to you!'

'I'm fine!'

'I didn't know that when I woke up in an empty bed, did I? And Jacob didn't know when he came into our bedroom to ask what was going on.'

'You didn't tell him what happened, did you?'

'No, but only because I had no idea myself at the time. But we'll have to tell him when we get home, won't we? I think he's going to notice that big black eye you've got. So what are you going to say to your son?'

That's a very good question and it's not one I have the answer to at present. We're going to have to have a serious conversation with Jacob very soon because this involves him, unfortunately. I was at that house fighting in his name, after all.

'I'll sort this out,' I tell Sara, but she isn't impressed with that answer, nor is she impressed with the fact that she has to drive me home because I'm still most likely over the drink-drive limit.

As we arrive back at our house, all I want to do is pop a couple of headache tablets, get into bed and sleep off this lousy hang-over, but that's not going to happen because Sara's friend, Shirley, is here, and there's an awkward encounter when she notices my black eye as I enter the house.

But it's not as awkward as when Jacob sees it. As he demands to know what happened, Sara thanks Shirley, who leaves but not without looking like she wishes she could stay and get all the gossip.

'Well, are you going to tell him?' Sara says to me, clearly still angry at me for going out on a one-man mission in the middle of the night.

'Erm, it's a long story, buddy,' I begin, wishing there was an easy way to say it.

'A long story that ends with your father being arrested.'

'Arrested! What did you do?' Jacob cries, looking totally aghast.

'I went to Mason's house,' I admit, and it's impossible not to feel a little sheepish as I confess to doing something wrong in front of him. It's usually the other way around in a father-son relationship.

'You did what?' Jacob looks mortified, which isn't good

because I've not even got to the part where I punched another person yet.

'I wanted to tell his dad what his son did to you. I thought it might help,' I say, but even as I repeat it, I know it was a stupid plan that was always unlikely to end well.

'Are you serious? Why can't you just stay out of it?' Jacob cries, furious.

'I'm not just going to stay out of it when you've been beaten up,' I say to defend myself, getting sick and tired of being the bad guy when I was only trying to do the right thing. 'I expected Mason's father to discipline his son for what he did to you and make sure it never happened again.'

'You should have known that wouldn't work by the way he was on TV after Zoe died,' Sara chips in, but I don't need her input at this time.

'Why did you do that? He's really going to hate me now!' Jacob tells me.

'Who?'

'Who do you think? Mason!' Jacob looks terrified, as if I've just put him on a collision course with a big, bad, scary monster, but that was not my intention, and I hate that he is so afraid of this boy.

'He's not going to hurt you now,' I try and reassure him.

'How do you know? You're not the one who has to see him at school!'

Jacob goes to run back up the stairs, but Sara has something to offer that might help.

'I'm going to go straight into the school on Monday morning and make sure Mrs Vigon knows exactly what Mason did to you,' she says. 'With any luck, they'll expel him, and you'll never have to see him again.'

'Are you stupid? That won't solve it! Of course I'll see him again. He lives in the same town as me!' Jacob cries, still despondent, and the slamming of his bedroom door a moment later brings an end to his contribution to this discussion.

'I'll go and speak to him,' I offer, but Sara stops me and inspects my black eye.

I stare into her clear blue ones as she examines me, but she's no medical professional so I'm not sure how valid her diagnosis will be.

'No, you're going to go and sit down, and I'm going to get you a bag of frozen peas to help with the swelling on your face,' she says, clearly opting for the tried-and-tested home remedy for when it comes to soothing swollen injuries.

'Does this mean you're not mad at me any more?'

'I didn't say I was mad,' she replies, which makes me chuckle. 'Just very disappointed.'

'I am sorry,' I say, meaning every word of it.

'I know you are. And I know you were just trying to do the right thing. Just please tell me you won't do anything like this again.'

'I won't,' I say, and Sara is happy with that answer because she leaves then to go to the kitchen and get those peas from the freezer.

As I take a seat on the sofa and try to rest my weary body, I can't help but feel uncomfortable about what I just said to my wife.

I assured her I wouldn't do anything like this again, and I wish I meant it.

But this is not over yet, far from it.

And as long as that's the case, who knows what else I'll have to do before things are right again.

THIRTEEN

SARA

I've never been so desperate for a Monday morning to come around this quickly, but it's finally here and it means I can go and speak to Jacob's headmistress again. However, I'm making the journey to my son's school alone because Jacob is not with me.

I decided that it might be best if he takes today off, just until I've had a chance to speak to Mrs Vigon and to allow a little of the dust to settle on what happened with Guy, Dean and Mason over the weekend. I don't know if Mason will be at school today, but it can't do any harm to keep my son out of that boy's way for a little while longer, at least.

I park amongst the vehicles that belong to the other parents who are dropping their kids off and the teachers who come here to work. The latter are easy to spot because they are the ones hurrying into the building with bags that are most likely filled with textbooks from last night's marking. I've never been able to comprehend how people can spend their childhood taking tests and then their adult life marking other people's tests, but I guess some people just love education. Either that or they like the generous school holiday allowance, but that's not for me to assume.

As I cross the playground, I think about how this is an unusual start to the week. I should be at my desk getting ready to start another day of work, but instead I'm here, trying to put out fires. I sent an email to Janice last night in which I told her I'd be starting a little later today and explained my reasons, only omitting the part about my husband getting into a fight with another parent, of course. Janice hasn't replied yet, but I'm sure she'll understand. She's a mother herself, so she should be able to appreciate my need to make sure my child is okay. If not, then I guess it's a matter for HR on another day.

I'm not the only one beginning the working week in an unusual fashion. My husband's Monday morning routine is all out of sync, too, because instead of being at his office, he's at home, lying in bed and still waiting for some of the bruising and swelling to go down around his eye. We both felt it was best if he avoided seeing anybody today, if only to stave off the inevitably awkward questions about what happened to him at the weekend. Guy joked that he'd just tell people he'd taken up boxing and ended up on the wrong end of a twelve-round war with some other gym buddy, but I reminded him this was not the time for jokes, so he soon shut up then. The fact he is even joking with everything going on says a lot, and makes me even more worried about whether the two of us are still compatible as we get older and our priorities change.

Trying not to dwell too much on the uncertain future in the long-term, I focus on the shorter term. Guy will probably go into the office tomorrow, just like Jacob will probably go to school, and for now, both the boys in my life are at home, safe and sound, while I'm out here trying to make their lives easier again.

The corridor that leads towards Mrs Vigon's office is crowded, and I have some difficulty passing through it easily, doing my best to avoid the army of uniformed schoolchildren that seem to surround me on all sides. I'm about halfway down when I hear somebody call my name and, as I turn, I recognise one face amongst the sea of youngsters. It's James, Jacob's best friend, and when he reaches me he asks if Jacob is with me.

'No, he won't be in today,' I tell him, touched that his friend is asking after him. James has been a good mate to Jacob ever since they became close in primary school, and I only wish all the other kids were like him. Mason could certainly do with taking a leaf out of James's book about how to behave towards his peers.

'Oh, okay,' James replies, but I wouldn't say he looks disappointed about that news. Rather, he looks very unsure. But it's not like James to be shy, so I ask him if everything's all right.

'Er, yeah, I better get to class,' he says before scurrying away, and I watch him disappear in the crowd, wondering what all of that was about. I don't have time though, because I have a headmistress to speak to.

When I reach her office, I make sure the receptionist knows that I'm here again.

It's funny, but I don't seem to have to wait as long as I did the first time, and as I enter the headmistress's office, I waste as little time getting to my point.

'Mason Burton attacked my son during a game of football on the playground at lunchtime last week, and I want to know what you are going to do about it.'

'Well, good morning to you too, Mrs Holdsworth,' comes the startled reply, but I've got no time for pleasantries.

'I'm sorry if I'm coming across as a little confronting, but how do you think I felt when I discovered severe bruising on my son's ribcage over the weekend? They are injuries he was given by another pupil here at this school. I thought our children were supposed to be safe here.'

'They are.'

'Oh, really? Do you want me to bring Jacob in so you can see just how safe he has been? Because I will. He can show you his ribs himself, and then you might change your mind.'

'Please try and calm down, Mrs Holdsworth.'

'I'll calm down when that boy is expelled from this school.'

'Mason Burton?'

'Yes!'

I wait with bated breath to see what Mrs Vigon will say to that, praying she will happily expel the child but also acutely aware that it's probably not going to be as simple as that. And sure enough, it isn't.

'I will speak to Mason this morning and get his version of events,' she promises me.

'And you really think he'll tell you the truth?'

'I'd like to think so, yes.'

'You really have no idea what kind of person you're dealing with here, do you?' I say, shaking my head in dismay. 'Mason Burton is not like the other children. He is a menace!'

'Like I said, I will speak to him, but if it's just his word against your son's, then...'

'It's not. The incident happened in the middle of a football match, so there were plenty of other pupils around. James Richardson was there for one, and there will be plenty of others. I can have Jacob give me their names. I'm sure they'll all have the same story about how Mason viciously kicked my son several times while he was lying on the ground.'

'Okay, well, we will get to the bottom of this. I'll need to speak to Jacob today.'

'He's not here.'

'Oh, why not?'

'Because I don't want him anywhere near that boy ever again. If you need to speak to Jacob, I can bring him in myself, or you can phone our house. But I don't want him here with Mason. It's just not safe.'

I leave the office having said my piece and hopeful that Mrs Vigon will conduct the necessary investigation and dish out the appropriate punishment. A boy like Mason isn't likely to have a clean record of behaviour at this school, so him beating up another pupil is surely enough to see him expelled. That's even before his previous history with Zoe is taken into account, and I have to think that will be the deciding factor if the headmistress is still sitting on the fence about what to do.

Satisfied that this should be over soon, at least from Jacob's perspective anyway, I leave the school and get back into my car to drive home, my route back to my vehicle made much easier now that all the pupils are in their classrooms. But there is still the matter of my husband and his situation with the police to sort out, and I guess that will be the next item on the agenda when I get back to the house.

I find Guy sitting in the kitchen gingerly eating a piece of toast, the bruising on his face looking just as bad as it did yesterday, so I guess the bag of frozen peas didn't work its magic like I'd hoped.

'How did it go?' he asks me as I enter the kitchen and put the kettle on, so I give him the quick rundown on my meeting with Mrs Vigon, and about how I made myself clear that Mason Burton had to leave that school, not just for Jacob's safety but the safety of every other child who goes there.

'Wow, it sounds like you really gave it to her,' Guy replies, looking impressed.

'Not everything has to turn into a fist fight,' I say to him before regretting my ill-timed joke, because I can see my husband is still very much in pain from his attempt at trying to sort out our son's problems himself.

'Maybe we should get somebody to have another look at

that,' I suggest as I take a closer look at the deep red circle surrounding his puffy eye.

'I'll survive,' Guy tells me before repeating his terrible joke about many a man having his head blown off and not moaning about it, a line he always trots out when someone in the family is under the weather.

At least he's still acting like himself, if not looking like himself, and I turn back to the kettle to carry on making my tea. Before I can reach for the sugar bowl, I hear the kitchen door crash into the wall behind me, and when I turn around, I see Jacob standing there with his phone in his hand.

'Look what you've done! I'm the laughing stock of the school now! And it's all your fault!'

'Woah, calm down, buddy. What are you talking about?' Guy asks, but Jacob just throws his phone onto the table and then storms out, leaving us very confused.

Guy picks up the phone to take a look, and when I join him I see a video on the screen. Guy presses play, and when it starts it takes us both a moment to realise what it is. But when we do, we both understand exactly why Jacob is so mad.

The footage is shaky and the lighting isn't great, but it's good enough to show us what we need to see and that is Guy punching Dean Burton before Dean gets the upper hand and proceeds to strike Guy several times and, on the face of it, clearly winning the fight. But it does show that Guy started it.

It also goes some way to explaining why Jacob is so distressed.

It looks like Mason's dad beat up his dad.

And that can't be a fun thing for the rest of the school kids to see.

Jacob must be feeling so embarrassed. I know I would be at his age if everyone in school was talking about me and the fact my father was having to fight my own battles for me. But that there is footage of the incident doesn't just make Jacob's life harder. It makes Guy's too, because now there is even more evidence against him for the police to take into consideration.

Why does it feel as if things keep getting worse? At what point will they get better for us?

Will things ever return to normal?

Or is it all downhill from here?

FOURTEEN

GUY

So now I am not only in trouble with the police, my wife, my son and possibly my employer, but I'm also going viral on the internet.

Life is nothing if not unpredictable, I suppose.

After seeing the video on Jacob's phone, I figured Mason must have got his own phone out and started recording just after his dad had pushed me away from their front door. In my desperation to hit Dean, I failed to see the camera recording over his shoulder and, because of that, I'm now all over the internet.

The video uploaded to Mason's social media account has thousands of views, clearly expanding out beyond this town and onto the phones of plenty of other teenagers, and possibly even their parents' too. With a title like 'My Dad Beat Up Someone Else's Dad – What A Laugh', the video was always bound to get plenty of attention from youngsters and parents alike, and I dread to think how many WhatsApp groups are now sharing this and having a good giggle about it, having come across it online.

It's easy to see why Jacob was so angry, because as far as he is concerned, everyone at his school has seen the video by now and will be laughing at me and, by extension, him, too. I can't say either Dean or I come off particularly well in the video, but considering it looks like I lost the fight, a fact my bruised face will attest to, means I am the sole butt of the joke. But perhaps more worryingly than that, it also means there is some solid evidence for the police to look at as they continue to conduct their investigation into what happened on Saturday night, and that is the last thing I need.

On second thought, I think I've spoken too soon because the last thing I actually need is my boss seeing that video and calling me into his office for a disciplinary hearing with HR, but that's exactly what happens ten minutes after I have arrived at work after my day off yesterday.

'This is not a good look for our company,' Archie, my sixty-year-old, super-stressed manager, says as he paces around the meeting room while Susan, the fifty-one-year-old, prim-and-proper HR Manager, sits in between, scribbling something down on a notepad. 'You can see how having one of our employees being involved in a fight that's all over the internet is a bad thing, right?'

'Yes, of course, and I'm very sorry,' I say, worrying that my job might be at risk now. Susan isn't here for nothing. Just what is she writing down on that damn notepad of hers?

'I can explain,' I say, hoping that a simple statement from me will put everyone's mind at ease. 'You see, my son was beaten up by that man's son at school. And you know who that boy is, right? It's Mason Burton, the one who bullied Zoe Atkinson into taking her own life three years ago.'

'Yes, we know who it is,' Susan says, suddenly chirping up. 'But that doesn't make it right. And it doesn't help us explain this to our shareholders.'

'Am I really that big a deal? I'm just a cog in the machine around here, aren't I?' I say, hoping my fairly bland and basic role as an auditor allows me some level of protection. It's not as if I'm the face of the company or anything like that.

'We take it seriously when any of our employees engage in unsatisfactory behaviour,' Susan tells me. 'Violence. Drug-taking—'

'I haven't taken any drugs!'

'But you have been involved in violence.'

'Outside the workplace and not with anybody here!'

'That doesn't matter. You're still a representative of this company. Then there's the matter of this being an issue for the police now. From what we have gathered, there is a criminal investigation underway. You are accused of assault, amongst other things. If found guilty, that could be considered a breach of your contract with us.'

'You're going to fire me?'

'We aren't going to make any definite decisions yet, but we have to make you aware that it is a possibility, yes.'

I can't believe this. Am I going to lose my job? I could handle losing face in public, but losing my income is another matter.

'So what's going to happen now?' I ask before burying my head in my hands.

I await the answer to my question nervously, but I don't get it right away because Archie and Susan tell me that they need to talk about this some more before they come to a decision. In the meantime, I'm told to work from home to avoid bringing any more attention here or distracting my colleagues from their own work.

'Again, I'm sorry, but I was just trying to defend my boy,' I say before I leave the meeting room, making sure to emphasise that point one more time, just in case it might help me when it comes time for them to make a final call.

I sheepishly make my way back to my desk, so I can gather up my things and leave as I've been told to do, but as I pass through the open-plan part of the office, I attract plenty of attention. It's hard not to stand out when you look like you've been in the ring with Mike Tyson, but not all of my colleagues simply gawk. A few of them approach me, and I'm surprised but relieved to find that they are all on my side.

'That family is a disgrace. Everyone knows it. It was about time somebody stood up to them.'

'If you see Dean Burton again, give him a punch for me.'

'Good on you, mate. I don't care what the police say, you're a hero. If that was my boy being bullied, I'd do the same thing.'

I accept a couple of handshakes and backslaps, but I decide it's best not to linger around for too long in case Archie and Susan are watching, so I break off from the crowd and go to my desk, before picking up my laptop and a couple of other necessary IT items, and making a sharp exit.

I spend the car ride home thinking about what I'm going to say to Sara. She already works from home herself, so it's impossible for me to get away with this and pretend like I'm still at my office. The thought does occur to me that I could take my laptop and try and work in a café, but even if the dodgy Wi-Fi somehow works for me there, the last thing I need is a bunch of strangers recognising me from that video online and gossiping about me even more. Best to go home and hide away, even if Sara will be there asking me why I'm not at work.

My presence at home is likely to only add further strain to our relationship at the moment. Not only does my partner think I've messed up in my personal life by getting into a fight with Dean while under the influence of alcohol, but now she'll know it's affected my professional life too.

I'm in desperate need of a victory, something to show her that I can help solve some of her woes rather than keep adding

to them. Unfortunately, I'm still scratching my head about how
I can make things better as I arrive home.

I park on our driveway and gather up my office equipment
before entering the house. I can hear Sara talking on the phone
in another room. I assume she's on a work call with Janice or
whatever her boss's name is, so I leave her to it and get busy
setting up a new workstation for myself in the kitchen. It might
suck that I'm being forced to do this, but trying to look on the
bright side, I no longer have to commute every day, and I'm now
working only a few feet away from all the snacks and bottles of
beer that are chilling in the fridge.

After spending ten minutes trying and failing to remotely
log onto my company's internal system, I am just about to make
a call to the IT Manager back at the office, when I hear Sara end
her call in the other room.

*Oh no, she's going to come and see me now, and this is the
part where I'm going to have to tell her that my job is at risk.*

I glance nervously at the fridge and wonder if it's too early
for me to open one of the beer bottles in there, but it's barely ten
thirty in the morning, so of course it is. Besides, there's no time
anyway because the kitchen door is opening now and, when it
does, Sara is standing there. But she doesn't look confused to see
me or angry. Instead, she looks very happy, and the big smile on
her face is a testament to that.

'What's going on?' I ask, puzzled, because I thought she
would have been the one to ask that question when she saw me.

'I have some good news,' she says, still smiling widely. 'I've
just got off the phone with Mrs Vigon, Jacob's headmistress, and
guess what?'

'What?'

'Mason Burton has just been expelled.'

It takes me a moment to process that before I find myself thinking about those beer bottles in the fridge again.

It's not too early to have a drink if there is something to celebrate, right?

That's certainly a piece of good news.

With Mason Burton now out of the picture, that's the end of our problems.

Isn't it?

FIFTEEN

SARA

'What happened?' Guy asks me after I've just told him about Mason's expulsion.

'Mrs Vigon spoke to some of the other kids that were involved in that football match, just like I asked her to, and they told her the same thing I did. Mason pushed Jacob to the ground and then kicked him in the ribs several times.'

'So that's it? He's out?'

'Yep, expelled with immediate effect. Mrs Vigon mentioned there being other things he'd already been on a watchlist for. Talking back to teachers, getting caught smoking once at the back of the school, not to mention his failing grades. It seemed this was the final straw.'

'Excellent! So Jacob won't have to see Mason Burton any more?'

'Nope.'

'Have you told him the good news yet?'

'No, I've only just got off the phone.'

'I think we should tell him now,' Guy says, sliding out of his seat at the table and joining me by the door.

Jacob is upstairs in his room, missing school for a second

day, after we decided the attention over the video he was so embarrassed about needed another day or two to die down. I told him that kids forget things quickly, and everyone will move on soon, but an extra twenty-four hours wouldn't do any harm, so he's still at home now. But he can go back to school tomorrow and even more so because the boy he was so worried about will no longer be there.

As Guy and I head up the stairs, I want to ask my husband why he is home when he should be at work, but one thing at a time, and as we reach Jacob's door, I knock a couple of times before walking in.

Jacob has barely spoken to either of us since he erupted so explosively yesterday in the kitchen, throwing his phone on the table and telling us it was our fault that he was the laughing stock of his school. We felt it best to let him simmer down before trying to engage too much again, but now we come bearing good news, I hope he will be more receptive to our advances.

'Get out,' Jacob says when he sees us, but we don't go anywhere, ignoring the loud video game on the TV as well as the dirty plates and used cups that are starting to pile up in the corner of his room.

'We've come to tell you that Mason Burton has been expelled,' I say, waiting for my son's face to light up. 'Mrs Vigon called me and told me just now.'

'What?'

So far, there is no smile on my son's face, but maybe he just needs a minute to process the news.

'He's gone. You won't be seeing that boy any more,' Guy says cheerily, and I bet my husband is enjoying the fact that Dean Burton hasn't come out of this as the big winner after all.

But Jacob is still not reacting to this in the positive way I would have imagined. Instead, he looks just as angry and afraid as he has over the last several days.

'What have you done? He's really going to hate me now!'

'It doesn't matter, you don't have to see him any more,' I say, echoing what Guy just told him. But it's of little solace to Jacob, who leaps up off his bed and almost knocks over one of the cups on the carpet.

'Just because he's not at school, it doesn't mean I won't see him!' he tells us, his voice loud. 'He's still around! Now he can just get me without any teachers to stop him!'

'What are you talking about?' I ask.

'The park. The bowling alley. On the street. He could still get his own back anywhere; it doesn't have to be on the playground!'

It breaks my heart that my son seems to be afraid of future reprisals extending out beyond the school gates, and I suppose I never really thought of it like that. But could it really be that bad? Jacob sure seems to think so.

'You don't get it, do you?' he cries. 'Things are different now, not like in your day. He doesn't have to wait for me at the school gates any more. He can attack me on social media where even more people will see it!'

'Maybe come off social media for a while then. Or just block him.'

'It's not that easy! All my friends are on there. Mason's mates are too, and they could keep posting about me even if he's blocked!'

Damn social media; Jacob is right, that was one thing we didn't have to concern ourselves with in our day. Back then, bullying began and ended in the school grounds, but now the internet is here, it's a whole other world.

'He can get my number and prank call me or make threats too,' Jacob says. 'Didn't you think of that?'

'If he makes any threats, then we will go to the police,' Guy says, but that does little to calm Jacob down.

'He can find out where I live. He probably knows already. What if he comes here? Or his dad?'

'Then we'll have the right to defend ourselves,' Guy tells him confidently. 'And anything they do, I'll make sure the police know all about it.'

But it's still not good enough for Jacob.

'Why did you have to do this? Why did you have to get involved?' he cries. 'You've ruined everything!'

'We've helped you,' I try, though it certainly doesn't look that way at the moment.

'Just get out!' Jacob tells us, and the venom in his voice is strong enough to shock us and see us both retreat into the hallway.

As Jacob slams his door closed behind us, I look at Guy and feel as hopeless a parent as I ever have.

'What did I do wrong?' I ask, desperately seeking answers from my partner, who looks just as shell-shocked as I feel.

'You didn't do anything wrong,' Guy replies before putting his arms around me.

'He hates us,' I say, stating the obvious. 'What if I have just made it worse for him?'

'No, you haven't. Mason deserved to be kicked out of school and now he has. It's not any of our faults that he behaved like he did, and after what he did in his last school, he never should have been allowed to end up at Jacob's.'

Despite my son's anger, I know Guy is probably right and try to take solace in the fact that I have acted like any worried parent would. What else was I supposed to do? Laugh off those bruises and tell my son to man up? Of course not. Mason deserved to be punished. If he committed that act on the street as an adult, then he would be punished, so why not as a school kid in the playground? If only he had been punished like an adult would have been over what he did to Zoe, none of us would be in this mess now.

We both decide to give Jacob some space, so we return downstairs. As Guy offers to make me a drink, I look at all his office equipment scattered about the kitchen table.

'Why are you working from home?' I ask him as he reaches into the cupboard for two cups.

'I was advised to do so by HR while they discuss the video that's been going around,' he says quietly.

'Why? Are you in trouble?'

'Maybe. Bringing shame on the company or something like that.'

'Did you tell them why you did it?'

'Of course. But you know what corporate types are like. They don't care about people's personal problems. They just hide behind legal talk and contracts.'

'Are you going to lose your job?' I ask, fear rising up in my throat as I contemplate our household income being halved overnight. We still have several years left on the mortgage on this place, not to mention helping out with Amber's university fees. And then there's the potential for Jacob to go on to higher education too, and we'd have to offer him the same financial support that his sister had if he does.

'No, I'm sure it'll be fine,' Guy replies, but he doesn't look at me when he speaks, so his answer carries little confidence.

'You need to go and speak to Dean and try and get him to drop the charges against you!'

'Speak to that guy again? You've got to be kidding. And even if I wanted to, the police have told me that I have to stay away from him.'

'But you have to try something!'

'It's too late now. Even if Dean did drop the charges, that video is still out there, and as far as the police will be concerned, it still shows evidence of a crime, so that's that. But Dean's not going to drop anything now, is he? Not after his son's been expelled.'

'Then what are you saying? You're going to go to prison?'

'No, that's not what I'm saying at all. It will all sort itself out in the end. Just try not to worry.'

'Try not to worry? Guy, this is serious!' I say, approaching him by the countertop and stopping him from distracting himself with the teabags.

'I know it is, but I'm going to sort it out, and everything will be okay,' he assures me. 'This will all be over soon.'

'Will it? Not if the police use that video as evidence against you. Not if you end up with a criminal record and lose your job. And not if our son still isn't safe from that boy, like he says he isn't.'

I feel on the verge of tears and could almost crumple to this tiled kitchen floor in a heap because I feel so overwhelmed by things all of a sudden. All I can do is reach out and hold the countertop beside me for support. It's not as if Guy is quickly on hand to offer me any support of his own. He is just standing there looking as helpless as I feel, which does absolutely nothing to improve my mood.

There's no denying I've been on a rollercoaster of emotions this morning, from thinking we'd won when Mason got expelled to suddenly fearing it's all going wrong with Jacob's anger and Guy's worsening job situation.

Maybe I simply won one battle.

But meanwhile, the war very much rages on.

SIXTEEN

GUY

Having spent the last couple of days working from home in a job I might soon be losing, trying to shield myself from what people might be saying about me and that video online, and anxiously awaiting an update from the police on their investigation into me, it's little wonder that I need some respite. But unlike the weekend, when I tried to find comfort in a bottle, I've decided to be a little more sensible this time, which is why I've decided to attend my weekly 5-a-side football game.

Perhaps exercise can help me clear my head and put a temporary halt to all the negative thoughts swirling around in there, and as I arrive at the pitches and see my friends conducting their warm-ups with a couple of footballs, I am glad I decided to come here.

Being teased and mocked in a light-hearted way by my closest pals might just be what I need, because there's nobody quite like mates to help somebody get over themselves and their problems by having a little perspective. Currently, my family life is a mess, so the burden of cheering me up is going to have to fall on my friends today, and they seem more than ready for that task as they see me walking over to them with a football under my arm.

'Here he is, the most famous man in the country,' Chuckles jokes in reference to the video of me fighting that is all over the internet.

'The country? I heard he's gone viral in China!' Fruit Loop quips. Despite being the butt of their jokes, I can't help but laugh.

'How did it feel to be trending on Twitter?' Baz asks me, pausing his set of keepie-uppies to ask the pertinent question.

'Twitter? I heard he's the newest star on TikTok!' Simmo shouts over as he chases down a loose ball, and I have no choice but to take it all on the chin, smiling at the banter and letting my mates get it out of their system before we can move on. This is just what I need. Some good-natured ribbing. It sure is a far cry from the heavy atmosphere that exists back at the house right now. But just to make sure I don't start thinking that my friends are completely against me, Baz stops messing around for a moment and has a quiet word with me.

'Joking aside, mate. How are you doing? We've been worried about you.'

'I've been all right,' I say, downplaying my recent struggles because that's what guys tend to do. 'It's not been easy, but I'm looking forward to running around and letting off some steam tonight with you boys.'

'Good to hear, mate,' Baz says as we prepare to get the game started against this week's opposition, who look to be younger than us, which doesn't bode well.

'Just try not to start any fights, yeah?' Chuckles jests, unable to resist making one more joke before the game gets underway.

As I had hoped, the combination of getting some exercise in the fresh air and being around my friends has done wonders for my mood, and after a hectic hour in which we fought valiantly but ultimately went down to a 4–3 defeat, I walk off the pitch with my teammates, smiling from ear to ear. I'm not sure how long the smile will last when I get back to the harshness of my real world very shortly, but for now, I'll take it.

Unfortunately, my smile is cut short even quicker than I anticipated when Fruit Loop gives me a nudge and tells me to look at who is waiting for me beside my car.

It's Kevin Atkinson.

He's wearing his football kit, so he must have been involved in a match on one of the other pitches tonight, and as I get closer I can see that he is definitely waiting for me because he gives me a wave as I near.

'You have a good game?' he asks me as I reach him, and the rest of my friends head to their cars around me, though they're all walking slowly and hoping to eavesdrop on the conversation I am about to have.

'Er, yeah, it was all right,' I reply, unsure why this man has bothered to make the effort to single me out for a chat.

'You're probably wondering what I want,' Kevin says, and I wonder if I've been rude by appearing more confused than I feel.

'Erm...'

'I heard about what happened with you and Dean Burton.'

'Oh, right. Yeah, I think everybody has.'

'Yeah, but not everybody has a history with that man like I do.'

That is true, and I wonder what Kevin makes of me punching the father of the son who bullied his late daughter.

'I just wanted to say well done. It's about time somebody stood up to that man and his family. Maybe if somebody had done so sooner, my daughter might be alive today.'

My friends have clearly heard how heavy this conversation has suddenly got because they all quickly get into their cars and start the engines, not wishing to hang around any longer. But I can't leave, not that I want to, especially after this man has just said something so personal.

'I'm sorry about what happened to your daughter,' I tell him, feeling a little of his pain but surely nowhere near the full extent of it. 'I probably shouldn't have punched Dean because it's got me in a load of trouble, but I just saw red. I guess I was expecting him to be different.'

'You mean you thought he would punish his son? There's no chance of that happening. Why do you think Mason is such a bully? It's because his dad is exactly the same.'

'Yeah, I guess.'

'What you did was no different to what countless people in this town have wished they had done. You did the one thing a bully doesn't like. You fought back.'

I watch as my friends' cars leave the car park and wonder how much more Kevin has to say to me. I guess he's finished because after he shakes my hand, he wishes my family and me all the best before turning to locate his own vehicle.

I almost let him go, but there's something so sad about him. The way he moves. The lack of energy. The fact that the light behind his eyes seems to have gone out. All of that, along with the fact that he never got the chance to try and save his child from the bullying ways of the Burtons, makes me feel so sorry for him, which is why I end up asking him if he would like to go for a pint on the way home.

He quickly accepts my invitation, and ten minutes later, we're sitting at a table in the pub across the road from the pitches, with two lagers and a packet of salt and vinegar crisps in front of us.

After ten minutes, we've made a bit of small talk about our football games tonight, as well as the décor in this pub and the noisy game of darts that is underway over in the corner.

However, we both know we're dancing around the elephant in the room, which is Mason, our children and the very serious consequences that can occur if bullying is allowed to continue unchecked. In the end, after half our beers have been supped and the crisp packet is empty, it's Kevin who touches on the delicate subject again.

'I know it might not feel like it at the moment but you're lucky,' he says to me as he stares into the frothy head of his beer. 'You found out that something was happening to your child, and you were able to do something about it. As for me, I had no idea Zoe was having any trouble at school. I didn't find out until I read the suicide note she left in her bedroom right before she...'

Kevin's voice trails off, but he doesn't need to finish his sentence. I put my hand on his shoulder and give it a firm squeeze, letting him know that he has my support, even though the two of us are hardly what we would consider to be friends. But, unlike how I am with my old mates, this is different. This is no time for joking around. This man is living a nightmare, and next to him my problems seem tiny in comparison.

'I tried my best to be a good dad,' Kevin goes on after I've removed my hand and he's taken a small sip of his pint. 'And I thought I was. But I couldn't see what was happening right under my nose. I missed how Zoe had started getting a little quieter, becoming slightly more withdrawn. How she wasn't finding quite as much joy in the things that used to make her happy. It all seems so obvious now when I think back on it but, at the time, I missed it all. I guess I had my mind on other things. Stupid things like work issues or what to watch on TV or whether or not Rovers might win the game at the weekend. I was so concerned with my own problems that I failed to see that Zoe had problems of her own.'

'It's not your fault,' I say, eager to try and cheer up my companion. 'You couldn't have known if Zoe hadn't told you. I only found out that my son had bruises because of a chance moment when he took his jacket off at a football match. If I hadn't seen that, who knows if I would have found out about it? You can't keep beating yourself up over what happened. The only person to blame is Mason.'

'He's not the only person, though, is he? His parents are to blame for raising a terror like that. And the teachers at Zoe's school? They should have seen he was bullying my daughter and done something about it. But nobody did. Not a single person took any of the blame for what happened, and, now she's gone, I feel my family are the only ones shouldering that blame.'

I rack my brain for something to say that might make him feel better, but I come up dry, at a complete loss for words. Fortunately, Kevin speaks again, relieving me of the pressure of finding something worthwhile to say myself.

'"You do whatever you have to do to keep your children safe",' he tells me, looking me in the eye so I can't fail to register how serious he is. 'Don't worry about the police or the general public or anything else. You just take care of your family because that's all that matters. You hear me? Don't end up like me, wishing I could turn back the clock. If you suspect anything is still going on with Mason or any other bully, you nip it in the bud as quickly as you can. And even if you don't suspect anything, make sure you keep a close eye on your son because he might just get better at keeping it hidden. Am I making myself clear?'

'Yes,' I say, nodding and feeling like I have to follow this man's advice as if my life, and potentially my child's life, depends on it, because judging by his appearance, it does.

'Good man,' Kevin says before picking up his pint again and taking another sip.

I guess that's the serious stuff over with now, so I quickly resume drinking my beer, too. Once we're finished, we both look like we're ready to leave.

'Thanks for the beer,' Kevin says to me as we leave the pub and walk back over to our cars.

'No problem at all,' I say, wishing I could do so much more for this man than simply buy him a drink.

He wishes me well, and I do the same to him before he gets in his car and drives away. But I'm a lot slower in leaving the car park, finding myself sitting behind the wheel and staring through my windscreen as I think about everything Kevin said and how seriously he meant it.

You do whatever you have to do to keep your children safe.

Those words are ringing in my ears, and they still are after I've eventually driven home, had a shower and got into bed beside Sara. I hear them over and over again as I fight for sleep, and even when I do drift off, I feel like I'm still hearing them some more.

I've really taken his message to heart and it's going to be a while before I stop thinking about those words.

By the time I did, it was already far too late to go back on what I'd done.

SEVENTEEN

SARA

Trying to concentrate on menial work tasks on a Friday afternoon is hard enough at the best of times, but it's even harder after the week from hell that I've just endured. Thankfully, as the clock continues to tick away in the bottom right-hand corner of my computer screen, I know that very soon there will be a brief bit of respite on the horizon. I'll finish work for today, as will Guy, and Jacob will be home from school. Then, with the three of us unburdened by our respective duties, there will be a little breathing space for us all to hopefully decompress in.

But we're not quite there yet because it's still only one o'clock, so there's a little way to go. For now, I'm in the house all by myself. Jacob will be with his classmates, which thankfully no longer include Mason, while Guy has just gone out to pick up a couple of grocery items from the supermarket that we can use for this weekend's meals. It's still not great that his boss is making him stay away from the office, pending the outcome of the investigation into his behaviour, but at least one good thing has come from it.

He can now do some of the chores that I usually end up getting lumbered with.

After whiling away another couple of minutes at my desk by displaying some seriously impressive procrastination skills, I go into full Friday-afternoon lazy mode by picking up my phone and checking my personal messages. When I do, I see there's one from Amber, my adventurous daughter, who has flown the nest but who has stopped having fun for long enough at university to at least message back her dear mother.

She tells me that she's had a busy week with lots of lectures and a couple of parties, although part of me suspects she's deceiving me slightly and it's more likely the other way around. But she seems in good spirits, which is all that matters. Well, that and the fact that she actually ends up getting her degree by the time she graduates, but that's a good couple of years away yet, so there's plenty of time for her to knuckle down and do some serious work before then. For now, I'm just glad she's having fun, making friends and, most of all, far enough away to not be stuck in the middle of all the drama going on back home. Of course, she's not completely immune to it all, because thanks to the video of her father in a fight being all over various social media feeds, she has seen it and knows that things are far from perfect in her family at present.

She phoned me as soon as she saw the video the other day and asked what was going on, worried about her dad, as well as the rest of us. I assured her we were all okay and it wasn't anything she needed to get in her car and come here to deal with. Lord knows at least one person in this family should be able to try and carry on as normal.

After typing out a reply to Amber in which I tell her that all is well back here (if she can tell me a white lie about the difference between the number of lectures and parties she is attending, then I'm sure I can get away with telling one of my own), I put my phone down and have another half-hearted go at doing some more work. Even then, I'm interrupted a moment later by somebody knocking on the front door, and as I get up from my desk to go downstairs and answer it, I suspect it is Guy, who must have forgotten to take his house key with him before heading to the supermarket.

I'm so busy wondering what potential treats he might have picked up while browsing the aisles that my daydream causes me to completely miss the fact that the silhouette on the other side of the frosted glass does not resemble his. It's only when I open the door and see who is standing on the other side of it that I am aware my husband is not back.

'Oh, so you are answering your door? I thought you'd have been hiding away in shame. You and your miserable excuse for a family.'

I stare at the woman on my doorstep, but once I've registered who it is, I can't say I'm surprised by her rudeness towards me. I am, however, surprised that she would show up here.

It's Mason's mum, Tracey.

'What do you want?' I ask, feeling a little nervous but doing my best not to show it.

'What do I want? Oh, how about an apology from you, for starters?' she says, and immediately, I can see where her son gets his confidence. This woman is not here to tiptoe around anything. But she's not somebody I'm keen to argue with based on how much bigger she is than me, though I'd guess that her size is less to do with any gym work and more to do with a poor diet. Either way, she's intimidating, though I am on home turf, and that means I feel I can defend myself if necessary.

'An apology? What for?'

'For getting my son kicked out of school! Does it make you feel proud that you've ruined a fifteen-year-old boy's education?'

'I've ruined it? I'd say he did a pretty good job of doing that all by himself when he decided to go around beating up other pupils!'

'Oh, come off it. He didn't beat anybody up.'

'Are you serious? So my son just got all those bruises on his ribs from nothing, did he?'

'It was a game of football on the playground. Kids tend to get a little bit rough with each other every now and then. What's the big deal?'

'The big deal is that my son was pushed to the floor and kicked several times, and if there hadn't been any other kids around to stop it, then who knows what damage could have been done by your animal of a son!'

'Who are you calling an animal?'

'Mason! And I'm calling you a bad mother!'

I should probably try and calm down, but I can't help it. I'm so angry that I've not only been ambushed at my own house but that this woman seems to think that what her son did to Jacob is perfectly acceptable.

'You've got some nerve!' Tracey says to me, clearly as furious as I am; but I refuse to back down because the red mist has well and truly descended over both of us now.

'And so have you! Your son is responsible for a little girl killing herself, and neither you nor your husband ever apologised for that! Let me guess, you don't think Mason was at fault there either, right?'

'Here we go again. Dredging up the past,' Tracey says, rolling her eyes. 'I will not have my son blamed for what that girl chose to do to herself. Not then and not now!'

'What she chose to do to herself? You mean committing suicide because your son had made her life such a misery?'

'So she couldn't handle school life. That's her problem. We all know kids can be tough on each other. It doesn't mean it's bullying.'

'Mason is a bully; there is no other word to describe him! Oh, wait, actually, there is. He's a coward too. Just like his parents!'

I'm well aware that I'm screaming myself hoarse right here, with my door wide open, so any of my neighbours who might be home can hear me. But I don't give a damn about that, and I'll carry on shouting at this woman if she won't take some responsibility for her son's actions or, better yet, get off my property and never come back.

'What am I supposed to do with my son's schooling now?' Tracey screams at me. 'He's got his GCSE exams next year but no school to take them in!'

'That's not my problem!'

'Well, I'm making it your problem!'

It seems there is no way this can end well because neither of us is backing down, and while it was our husbands who ended up in a fistfight before, there's every chance we might just be about to do the same thing. That is until we hear the sound of a car approaching, and as I look past Tracey I see that Guy is back.

She sees him too, and as he parks on the driveway she quickly makes her exit, rushing away before my husband has a chance to turn off the engine and get out of his car. Before she goes, she has one more thing to say, and she makes sure I hear it by shouting again, as well as jabbing her finger in my direction for good measure.

'This is not over! Do you hear me? Not over! You and your family better watch your backs!'

'Hey, what the hell is going on?' Guy asks as he gets out from behind the wheel, but Tracey ignores him, already well away down the street and not looking back, even with me shouting after her *to get lost and never come back to my house again.*

I'm physically shaking as Guy reaches me in the doorway,

and it takes several long minutes for him to help me calm down. Once I have, there is only one thing I am going to do, and with Tracey's warning still ringing in my ears, I pick up my phone and dial a very simple series of numbers: 999.

EIGHTEEN

GUY

As if this week couldn't get any worse, there are now two police officers sitting in my living room across from Sara and me. They are here after Tracey Burton came to visit us, and while I still don't know every single thing that was said between my wife and that woman about an hour ago, I am about to get the full rundown now. That's because the police want to hear it all, and my wife seems more than willing to share that information with anybody who will listen.

'She's crazy!' Sara says for the fourth time since Tracey left, and the second time since the police arrived. 'She's actually psychotic! They all are! Her, her husband and her son, and you need to do something about them because this is getting worse, not better!'

I think about politely advising Sara to try and calm down a little bit, if only because shouting at police officers is never normally a sensible way to behave, but then I remember the last time I suggested such a thing. My wife did not take too kindly to the words 'calm down', and I doubt much will have changed if I was to try again. That's why I decide to simply sit beside her, and when one of the police officers looks in my direction, I simply give them a look that says, 'I've tried.'

But it's also not fair to assume that Sara can just simmer down. Not after what she just experienced, and while I hate that she had to be the one to deal with the full force of Tracey Burton's anger, it might have been a blessing in disguise that it was her and not me. I missed nearly all of it, but if I had been the one to open the door to Tracey, things might be even worse than they are now.

I didn't exactly cover myself in glory during my last dealings with that family, did I? And now it's those dealings that the police officers seem to want to focus on.

'I believe there was an incident between you and Mr Burton, is that correct?' PC Finch asks me, the older and shorter of the two men who have been assigned to this particular job today out of all the other possible police officers who might have been sent here. I wouldn't say they've drawn the short straw, but I wouldn't say they've been blessed with a great job to do, either.

'Er, yes, but that is a separate matter,' I say. 'It shouldn't have anything to do with this one.'

'Well, maybe in an ideal world, yes, but if we're being realistic, then I'd say it is obviously connected,' Finch tells me, possessing the type of common sense that I was perhaps cheekily hoping he might not. 'You have a history with the Burton family. It seems that all of you do, and this is just another footnote in that history.'

'A footnote? Are you calling me being threatened on my own doorstep a footnote?' Sara cries, losing her temper as easily as PC Finch strokes the stubble on his chin.

'Please, I'm not trying to downplay what happened to you or make light of it,' Finch says as his colleague beside him looks awkwardly on. 'I'm simply saying that Mrs Burton's behaviour did not come out of the blue. It is most likely retaliation for what has happened with her son's expulsion from school and her husband's injuries when he was struck on his own doorstep.'

'I was struck too!' I say, making sure that is remembered, though neither officer deems it worthy enough to jot down in their notepad, probably because they already know that I was the one who threw the first punch, so anything after that could be considered self-defence.

'That investigation is still ongoing,' PC Fox chips in, showing that he has been listening this whole time and has finally decided to do some of the work his chattier colleague has so far been fielding. 'Charges are still pending, and, as advised, you are to stay away from the Burton home until there is an outcome.'

'Yes, I know that,' I reply, wishing PC Fox would go back to being quiet again. 'But they came to us this time, so we wish to press charges against them now!'

'Charges of what?' Finch asks.

'Harassment! Abuse! Making threats!' Sara says, getting up from her seat, though I make sure to quickly reach out and take her hand so she can't get too animated and start getting into the officers' faces. 'She told me this wasn't over and that we should watch our backs! Is that enough for you to take this seriously?'

That is something that the officers deem worthy of writing down in their notepads, and I guess we're finally getting somewhere but still not as fast as either my wife or I would like.

'We will go and speak to Mrs Burton,' Finch tells us, which is obviously the least they can do, although I decide not to point that out just yet. 'And we will get her version of events.'

'She's hardly likely to tell you the truth, is she?' Sara cries. 'I very much doubt she'll admit to threatening me to two police officers.'

'Maybe so, but we have to let her have her say,' PC Fox reminds us.

'And then what?' I ask. 'She'll be taken to the police station and charged like I was?'

'It might not be as simple as that,' Finch tells me before sighing a little too heavily. 'Were there any other witnesses to this? Third-party, impartial witnesses, I mean? Anybody who could verify what Mrs Burton actually said to you, because otherwise, this could be a case of he said, she said, or in this case, she said, she said.'

I'm not sure if PC Finch is making light of this or if he's just very unaware of how he might be coming across as a little uncaring, but either way I don't appreciate it. Fortunately, Sara is on hand to not let that bother her.

'Ask my neighbours. One of them should have heard. She was screaming at me. I'd be surprised if they couldn't hear her over on the next street.'

'We will go and knock on a few doors,' Fox says. 'Although I'm not sure how many people will be home in the middle of a working day.'

I silently think to myself about my neighbours and which of them might have been home when Tracey came rudely knocking, but other than Mrs Granger, the elderly woman at Number 22, I'm not sure. The rest of the residents are like us, young families where the parents work and the kids are in education. Maybe, unfortunately for us, nobody heard what happened.

'Hopefully, this disagreement between your two families will simmer down in time,' Finch says as he and his colleague stand to leave. 'In the meantime, I'd implore you not to do anything that might further inflame things.'

'We are not the ones inflaming things,' Sara reminds them, and I quickly back her up.

'Yes, we just want to be left alone. Our son was quite happy at school before Mason Burton gave him trouble, and my wife and I were quite happy in our lives until we had to deal with that family.'

That last sentence might not be strictly true because I wouldn't say things between us have been perfect, but telling a white lie strengthens my argument and helps drive home my point a little more, so I'll go with it.

'Okay, we will be in touch when we have spoken to Mrs Burton, as well as some of your neighbours,' PC Fox says as they leave our house, crossing over the same doorstep where Tracey Burton said her piece so aggressively only a short time ago.

How I wish my son had been on hand to record the incident like Dean's son had been when I was on his doorstep, because then we would have hard evidence like they did. We could also embarrass that woman online like her family embarrassed me. But there was no camera and unless we get lucky with the neighbours, no witnesses at all, which means as Sara and I watch the police officers walking up our street, we can only hope that someone will support us.

But as long as the police are being proactive, then that is all we can wish for. Who knows, they may find a witness or Tracey Burton might just be honest and relay everything she said to them. Better yet, we might get lucky in that this was the final thing to happen between our two families, and this is the end of the matter. Perhaps Tracey just had to have that one blowout, just like I did when I went to her house. But her being questioned by police will surely be as sobering an experience for her as it was for me and, therefore, might just be the thing that gets her to leave us alone.

Wishful thinking?

Possibly.

But as Sara and I close our front door and try to get on with the rest of our day, it's about the best we have at this time. Surely things can't get any worse from here. We've all said our piece and some of us have gone even further than that. But that has to be it now, doesn't it?

How much further could this go?

Unfortunately, the answer to my question was not a positive one.

Instead of this war between two families being over, it would soon turn out that it had barely even begun.

NINETEEN

SARA

A week has passed since Tracey Burton came to see me so unceremoniously, and despite very little happening in terms of her and the police inquiry into her behaviour, I am pleased to say that just as little has happened in all other areas. Jacob is happier again and is having no more problems at school now Mason has gone, while neither I nor my husband have had any further dealings with that boy's parents. It seems some normality has returned, and I'm very grateful for that, because while some might say the quiet life is boring, I'd take it any day over all the drama we've had in the last few weeks.

While the police weren't able to find anybody who witnessed Tracey's verbal assault on me, meaning there's not much they can do there, I'm pleased her threat of this not being over seems to have come to nothing. I have no idea what Mason Burton is doing now and whether or not his parents have managed to find a new school that will take him, but that's not my concern. I only care about my son, and all that matters there is that Jacob is back to his old self again, and by that I mean he's not whiling away all his free time by spending it cooped up in his bedroom.

When he's not been at school or attending any extra-curricular sports clubs, he's been sitting with us downstairs, watching TV and chatting away like always. And now it's the weekend, I get further proof that the real Jacob is back because he tells me that he is off out to go and meet his friends for a game of football at the local park.

'That sounds good,' I tell him before enquiring as to what time he might be back so I'll know when to arrange our evening meal.

'I don't know, maybe six,' he tells me, so I make a mental note to prepare the food for around seven, because Jacob has never been one to accurately stick to times when he's going out with his friends, and often comes back later than advertised.

As I wave him off and watch him disappear down the driveway with a ball under one arm and a bottle of sports-energy drink in hand, I smile to myself for a couple of reasons.

One, I know my son is happy again.

And two, my husband and I now have the place to ourselves for the afternoon.

Not wanting to waste a single second of this unexpected but happy occurrence, I rush out to the back garden, where Guy is busy cutting the grass, a job I assigned to him earlier when I noticed that the sun was out and the garden was looking a little neglected. My husband reacted as he always did to the suggestion of such a chore, tutting, sighing but ultimately going ahead and getting on with it, and I was pleased to see that. But that was back when I thought Jacob might be under our feet all day. With our son gone, I might consider giving my man a slightly more fun way to spend his Saturday afternoon.

He's unable to hear me over the sound of the mower, but I soon get his attention when I pull the plug out, and while he turns around and initially looks annoyed to have been disturbed, he soon starts smiling when he sees the look on my face. It's a look I call 'The Sexy Suggestion', and that look, coupled with me teasing him by not only winking but running a hand very slowly down the front of my blouse, soon has him rushing across the freshly maintained grass to find out what is going on. When he reaches me, I plan to make it even clearer that I am hoping we can do a little maintenance on our marriage as well, after recent events have strained things between us and taken us both a little further away from where I feel we both need to be.

'Jacob's gone out to have some fun,' I tell Guy as I admire the small beads of sweat that have formed on his forehead thanks to all the manual labour he has been doing for me. 'I was thinking maybe we could have a little fun of our own as well?'

My husband might not be the sharpest knife in the drawer, but even he can't fail to miss that hint, and as he follows me inside the house, I decide to make a quick stop off in the kitchen to pick up the bottle of white wine that I know is chilling in the fridge. It's a bottle I was saving for this evening, but that was before I suddenly saw the opportunity to let my hair down and de-stress a little earlier after recent events. As I retrieve the bottle, Guy is already on the same page, opening a cupboard to find a couple of wine glasses.

Neither of us has to drive later today, so indulging in a little alcohol in the afternoon will not pose a problem. We head upstairs, and I smile at the sound of my fingernails clinking slightly against the side of the cold bottle. I smile even more when Guy opens that bottle in the bedroom and pours us both a glass before we take a long and satisfying sip and toast a 'cheers' to ourselves. Neither of us has to elaborate on that, but we both know it's done to signify how we have stuck together through this recent testing time, and come through it on the other side with the most important things still intact, those things being our son's happiness and our love for one another, after both have been pushed to breaking point lately.

We spend the next hour proving that love to each other in

all manner of strenuous ways, and by the time I'm savouring my second glass of wine, the bedroom floor is littered with my clothes, and the beads of sweat on Guy's forehead are more prominent than they were earlier.

'Wow, I thought I'd have to wait for Jacob to go to university like his sister before we got to spend our Saturday afternoons like this,' he tells me with a laugh.

'Don't get too comfortable. You still need to finish cutting that grass,' I quip, and he makes sure to tickle me to show me what he thinks of my teasing.

'I don't think it's safe for me to operate a lawnmower now that I'm under the influence of alcohol.'

'You might be right. Is it considered drink-driving if you cut the grass while drunk?'

'I don't remember seeing any gardening shows in which the host was tipsy.'

'That's a fair point. Maybe leave the grass until tomorrow, then.'

'Won't Jacob get suspicious if he comes back and sees that I didn't finish?'

'He's not that observant,' I remind him, and we chuckle at our son's lack of observation skills before we start kissing again.

The next couple of hours are spent in bed with only a couple of wine-induced toilet breaks interrupting us, but when I see the clock approaching five, I think it might be time to get up, just in case Jacob surprises us and comes back earlier than planned. But Guy is far too relaxed now, never mind inebriated, to worry about such a thing, so he makes sure to keep me under the duvet for as long as possible. But it seems we have delayed things too long when I hear a key in the front door ten minutes later.

'Damn it! He's back early!' I say, leaping out of bed and scrabbling around for my clothes, hoping to get myself covered up before Jacob can make it upstairs and figure out what's been going on while he's been with his friends.

Guy is just as eager to make himself look more decent, and as the pair of us run around the bedroom like a couple of naughty teenagers and not the grown adults we are, we can't help but giggle at this turn of events. However, that giggling stops when we hear Jacob running up the stairs, because it sounds like he's in a rush and, if so, he might just catch us before we're dressed.

That doesn't end up happening because I hear a door slam, and while at first I think he's gone back into his bedroom, it's only when I go out into the hallway that I see it was actually the bathroom that he just entered.

Both now appropriately dressed, Guy and I share a confused look before I call out to Jacob to see how he is.

'Everything okay?' I ask him, but there's no response.

'Jacob? You okay, buddy?' Guy tries, but again, there's nothing.

Neither my husband nor I need reminding that this is very reminiscent of how Jacob behaved back when he was having trouble at school not so long ago. Eager to avoid further repeats of that, I approach the bathroom quickly, to hopefully nip whatever it is in the bud as soon as possible.

'Jacob, what's going on?' I call out, giving my son one last chance to tell us that he just needed to use the toilet quickly and everything is actually okay. He still doesn't reply, leaving me with little choice but to try and open the door myself.

But the door is locked.

'Jacob! Either answer me or open this door!' I cry, starting to panic a little, and Guy is soon by my side, trying the handle for himself before knocking loudly on the door and urging it to be opened as well.

'Jacob, you're scaring us!' Guy says, genuine worry in his voice as he keeps trying to get some response from the bathroom, and now both our minds are running wild with what new horrible thing could be troubling our child. It's only when we hear the sound of Jacob coming out that we get a true sense of the nightmare that is unfolding.

The door opens, and our son allows us to see him for the first time since he got home.

When we do, it's hard to even recognise the person we are looking at for a moment.

All we can see is blood.

TWENTY

GUY

Can there be anything more horrifying for a parent to see than their own child covered in blood? That's precisely the sight that Sara and I are forced to lay our eyes on when Jacob eventually emerges from the bathroom and, when he does, nothing could have prepared me for the shock of what I'm witnessing.

Jacob's features are covered in open wounds that are leaking onto the bathroom floor by his feet. His forehead, cheeks, neck and ears are bloodied, and there's even some crimson in his hair. The front of his football jersey is splattered with red, while there's blood on his hands, too, as he keeps wiping his face in a futile bid to clean himself up.

Only his legs seem to have avoided becoming bloodied, but they are not entirely unscathed because there are several patches of mud smeared across his knees just below his shorts, which also have mud on them. His trainers are just as muddy, but that's not what is bothering us as he continues to stand there and make a mess on our floor.

The blood is clearly the most troubling part of this whole scene.

'What the hell happened?' I cry, hoping that this is all just some strange nightmare I'm having after I drank too much wine this afternoon with Sara. Maybe I'm still in bed now, having fallen asleep after drinking too much. That would be great because it would mean this isn't actually happening after all.

The problem is, I feel very much awake.

'Jacob!' Sara shouts after he has failed to answer me, and despite the state of our son, she has no qualms about touching him and getting blood all over her own clothes too.

'What is it? Where are you hurt?' Sara says, trying to figure out from where exactly the blood is coming. But that's the problem. It seems to be coming from everywhere.

'Get off me,' Jacob says, but his voice is quiet, and he's not completely dismissive of his mother's attention, because he doesn't pull away and try to close the bathroom door again. If anything, he looks shell-shocked, and I can't blame him.

He looks like he's been in a war.

Has he?

'What happened? Did you fall over?' I try, simply guessing, but what else can I do?

Jacob doesn't reply as Sara tentatively touches his face, her hands now just as red as her son's.

'Oh my gosh, you poor thing. We need to get you to the hospital,' she says, but Jacob protests, pushing her hands away and telling us that he is fine. It's an absurd thing to say given his appearance, but it's made even more ridiculous by the fact that when he speaks, I can actually see one of his teeth wriggling in his gum.

I can't imagine the pain that is causing him and I suddenly feel queasy, the sight of the loose tooth seemingly the final straw, but my desperation to find out exactly what happened overpowers any nausea I might be battling at present.

'Jacob, tell us what happened. Now!'

My raised voice startles him and Sara, but it's time to get

serious. It seems to work because Jacob is just about to speak, but before he does, I hear a knock at the front door.

I consider ignoring it, but as Sara goes back to trying to tend to our son's wounds, I give up waiting for an answer on what might have happened to him and rush downstairs, hoping that whoever is at the door might be able to enlighten me. And fortunately, they can.

James, Jacob's best friend, is on the doorstep, clearly out of breath, and while he's looking a hell of a lot better than his mate currently is, I notice there is some blood on his hands and clothing too.

Did these two have a fight? Hopefully not, or this is one friendship that is almost certainly over.

'Is Jacob here?' James asks me, and the concern in his voice makes me think that he might not be the culprit of my son's injuries after all.

'Yes, what the hell happened to him?'

'He was beaten up at the park!' James replies and, as he does, I see a couple more of Jacob's friends arriving at the end of my driveway, each of them looking like they have just sprinted to get here almost as quickly as James has.

'What?'

'He was beaten up!'

'Who by?'

'Mason Burton!'

The mention of that boy's name again sends a shiver down my spine.

'Mason did this to him?' I ask through gritted teeth.

'Yeah,' James replies before the rest of the group makes it to the doorway, and while I recognise all the boys here, the one I want to see is conspicuous by his absence.

'Where the hell is Mason now?' I ask, wishing I could get my hands on that boy, because if I could, there would be even more bloodshed today.

'He ran off. We tried to catch him, but he got away,' says Andy, another of Jacob's mates from school, and whose father I have enjoyed a couple of beers with in my time.

'How did this happen?' I say, glancing behind me to see if Jacob has come downstairs, but he's nowhere to be seen, perhaps unsurprisingly, because who would want their friends to see them like that?

'We were playing football in the park,' James tells me. 'We'd been there for a while, taking it in turns to be the goalkeeper. When it was Jacob's turn, the ball went over the crossbar and into the bushes behind him. He went to get it, but he didn't come back.'

'We called out to him, but he didn't answer,' Andy says, taking over the telling of the story. 'So I went to try and find him. I thought he might be struggling to find the ball in the bushes or something. But when I got there, I saw him on the floor, and Mason was on top of him, punching him in the face.'

'He was doing what?' I say, fighting the anger that is rising up inside of me.

'He was on top of him, and he wouldn't get off, even when I called out to him to stop,' Andy goes on. 'So I called the other guys over to help me, and then I ran towards Mason to get him off. He hit me too.'

Andy turns his cheek, and I can see a red mark on the side of his face, though considering the extent of my son's injuries, I'd say Andy got off very lightly in comparison.

'Mason ran away then, but before we could check on Jacob, he ran away too,' James says. 'I figured he was running home, so we came after him. We wanted to see if he was okay.'

'No, he's not okay. Far from it,' I tell him, my heart thumping in my chest almost as hard as I imagine Mason was thumping my son earlier. 'We need to get him to a hospital.'

I leave the boys at the door then and rush back inside, calling out to Sara to find out what's going on up there. She doesn't reply, so I run upstairs and find her with Jacob, leaning over the sink and trying to stem the flow of the bleeding from some of his cuts as a lot of red liquid drips into the sink.

'Your friends just told me what happened,' I say to Jacob. 'About Mason Burton. He did this, didn't he?'

Jacob doesn't say anything or even acknowledge the question.

'Jacob?'

He finally nods his head as Sara dabs at his nose with some tissue paper.

'Right, that's it, that boy is in serious trouble now,' I say, turning back to the bathroom door, fully on the warpath.

'Wait. What are you going to do?' Jacob asks me, seemingly still terrified of his attacker and proving just how naive Sara and I are by thinking that we had managed to successfully keep him safe.

'Don't go to his house,' Sara begs me, clearly afraid that I'll get myself into more trouble with the police. But I'm not going to be that stupid this time.

'I'm not going to his house; I'm going to get the phone, so I can call the police, and they can come here and see exactly what Mason Burton is really capable of,' I say. 'And I'll be calling for an ambulance too.'

'Dad, wait!' Jacob tries, but I ignore him as I rush into our bedroom and pick up my phone from the bedside table.

As I dial 999, I look at the empty bottle of wine beside the bed, as well as the two glasses and the twisted bedsheets that Sara and I were lying entangled in not so long ago, and while it had been a fun afternoon, the sight of it all now makes my stomach turn. That's because I know that while we were drinking and sleeping together, our poor son was getting beaten senseless behind some bushes at the park, and it was so bad that even his friends couldn't help him. Talk about the afternoon taking a very dramatic U-turn, so much so that my head is spinning and I'm almost feeling as dazed and confused as my son must be from the blows he took from Mason.

I thought everything was back to normal.

How could this have happened?

By the sounds of it, Mason was waiting in those bushes in the park to ambush Jacob when he got the chance and, boy, did he get that chance. But as the call connects and the operator asks me which emergency service I require, I know this is my chance too.

It's my chance to have that boy and his family punished properly and, like Zoe's father would agree, punished like they should have been a long time ago.

That's why I'm going to make sure I take it.

This is where their luck runs out.

TWENTY-ONE

SARA

It was one thing to see the police officers come back to our house again, but it was quite another to see them joined by a team of paramedics this time, and as the ambulance parked up and medical assistance was finally administered to my son, I couldn't hold off the tears any longer.

Sobbing into Guy's shoulder, I tried and tried to pull myself together, but it was impossible. Seeing Jacob being fussed over by emergency workers, as well as knowing how much he was in pain, both physically and mentally, no doubt due to the embarrassment of being beaten up in front of his friends, was simply too much for me to bear. I know it was just as hard for my husband, too, though he managed to avoid crying in front of everybody. But whenever I looked into Guy's eyes, I saw something just as disturbing as tears.

I saw a rage burning, and it was a rage that no amount of reassurance from the police or ambulance crews could put out.

After initially being checked over at the house, it was decided that Jacob should go to the hospital to receive further treatment for his various injuries, so he was put into the back of the ambulance, although only after we had to persuade him.

Insisting that he was fine and just needed to be left alone, Jacob eventually conceded and did as the medics asked of him, though he only got into the ambulance once he was assured that his friends were no longer waiting outside.

That took a little while to arrange because the police were keen to speak to the youngsters and get the witness accounts of what happened at the park, but once that was done, Guy thanked James, Andy and the rest of our son's friends and told them we would be in touch with them soon once we had an update at the hospital. Then he asked them to leave, telling them it would be easier for Jacob to come back outside and show his face again if he knew all his school pals wouldn't be there to gawk at him.

Once the boys had left, I went with Jacob into the back of the ambulance, and the pair of us were driven to the hospital alongside a paramedic who continued to care for him on the way. Guy followed behind in his car, as did a couple of police officers, and once we reached our destination, things felt as if they became even more real then.

Being in an environment of operating theatres full of stern-looking surgeons and passing wards full of puce-looking patients brought home just how serious this was, not that we needed that reminder. But hospitals have a funny way of bringing any picture into a sharper focus, and it certainly did that for Guy and me as we were spoken to by a nurse who gave us the rundown of what we could expect to happen to Jacob over the next several hours.

The first item on the agenda was to make sure his wounds were treated, sterilised and stitched up so no further blood loss could occur. But that was only the superficial stuff, and there was much more that needed to be done once the flow of blood had been stopped. There would have to be X-rays to check for broken bones, and the fact that one of Jacob's cheeks was extremely swollen suggested there was at least a fracture somewhere underneath all the surface-level damage. There would also be a CT scan, the best outcome of which would hopefully just be a concussion.

There would have to be some emergency dental work done to the broken teeth in our boy's mouth, the pain of which was giving Jacob the most discomfort of all, and would mean it was unlikely he would be able to eat solid foods for a while. And, as well as that, the rest of his body would need to be examined, because while his head had clearly borne the brunt of the vicious attack, there did seem to be potential injuries elsewhere, the most obvious evidence when Jacob had been limping as he got into the ambulance. Quite how he managed to run home from the park if his legs were hurt shows just how much the adrenaline was racing inside his frightened body.

And then, on top of all that – but only once the physical stuff has been dealt with – there would come the reparations to his fragile mental state. Quite how anybody will process being beaten savagely is beyond me, but a fifteen-year-old boy? There's no doubt that Jacob is going to require some kind of therapy, even if it is just to make sure that he really is okay when he says he is, because he could just be lying and wearing some deep scars in his psyche, just as much as he is on his face.

All of that adds up to a fairly long road to recovery for our son, beginning in this hospital but ending god knows how far down the line, if and only if he ever gets back the confidence that such an attack will have robbed him of. And all of that is why I am finding it impossible to stop thinking about the boy who did this to our son, and how there are so many ways I want him to pay for this crime, not all of which are entirely legal.

I know Guy feels the same way, because when he hasn't been with me, he's been out in the hospital corridors, either talking to more police officers or simply pacing up and down with a strained look on his face. I can see that this is killing him, though I feel exactly the same way, and while it can't compare to what Jacob is going through, there's no doubt that Guy and I have some recovering of our own to do after this.

But it's far too early for any of that, because, right now, the only thing either of us wants is to see Mason Burton arrested and punished to the full extent of the law. Although, once again, his tender age might be the thing that helps him avoid ever really paying the full price for his sins. He's a minor, so he can't be punished like an adult can. But he can still be punished, right? That depends, and we get the first hint of that when a police officer with wispy blonde hair and a slight under-bite comes to tell us that Mason has been questioned in the presence of his parents before being released.

'Why have you let that son of a bitch go?' Guy wants to know, ready to start pacing all over again. I swear if he had a pedometer on him, he'd have easily done over ten thousand steps since Jacob was first admitted here.

'It's just on bail, and it doesn't mean he isn't going to be charged with anything,' the officer tries to assure us, though after all that's come before, his words give us little confidence.

'What will happen when you find him guilty?' I ask, assuming they will find him so, because surely the evidence speaks for itself in this case.

'If that's the case, then he will be sentenced in a youth court, and the punishment will be subject to several things.'

'Like what?' Guy snarls, pausing briefly before starting to pace again.

'Well, they will take into consideration all manner of things. His age and level of maturity being the first.'

'If he's old enough and mature enough to viciously beat somebody up, then he's old enough and mature enough to face the consequences,' I tell the policeman, and Guy is quick to agree.

'Then there is the seriousness of the accused offence,' the officer goes on, clearly not wishing to dwell on what I've just said. 'And whether or not the suspect admits that offence, which, as of yet, he has not.'

'I don't care if he tries to pretend he didn't do it,' Guy says, clenching his fists and shaking his head. 'Several people can attest to the fact that he was beating the hell out of my boy, so he can deny it all he wants, but there are witnesses to this crime.'

'The youth court will also consider any previous history of offences in the case of the accused.'

'Well then, I'd say it's a slam dunk because Mason Burton is guilty of a hell of a lot in his past,' I cry, clenching my own fists now. 'He's recently been expelled from school because he attacked my son during a football match at lunchtime, so how about that for previous? And then there is what he did to Zoe Atkinson, bullying her, for which he was also expelled, but that's the least of it. That poor girl killed herself because of what he did. Do you think that's enough of a history to form a good enough picture of what Mason Burton is like?'

I'm out of breath and need to calm down, but I won't do so yet. Not until the person who hurt my son both physically and mentally is behind bars somewhere, whether it be a youth detention centre or another place more befitting of the adult crimes he seems old enough to perpetrate.

'And lastly, the youth court will take into consideration the family circumstances,' the policeman tells us, and it's a statement that instantly troubles my husband.

'What the hell do you mean by the family circumstances?'

'Well, as the accused is a minor, his home life will be examined, or, more specifically, the character of his parents and the role they have played in his upbringing, both recently but also historically.'

'What has that got to do with anything?' Guy snaps back. 'His parents are trouble themselves; there's no doubt about that, but they haven't got anything to do with what their son did.'

'That will have to be determined.'

'What does that mean?' I ask, starting to worry there might be yet another loophole coming here that will see Mason Burton get away with what he's done.

'The court will have to ascertain if the accused has been subjected to any similar incidents himself. Violence, domestic abuse. It doesn't have to be against him specifically; it just may be that he has witnessed it occurring to other people, which will have had an impact on him if so.'

'You're saying that if his mum and dad beat him up or if they beat up each other and he's seen it, then Mason might have an excuse for his behaviour?'

'Not an excuse as such, but it might go some way to explaining why somebody his age has allegedly committed such a violent act against another person.'

'That would be awful if he has seen such things,' I say because of course it would be. 'But that still doesn't make it right, does it? It doesn't give him licence to beat somebody up or bully a twelve-year-old girl into killing herself! His parents didn't do those things, he did!'

'Yeah, damn right,' Guy chips in. 'And I can already tell you that Mason saw his father beat me up at their house not so long ago, but even then, Dean did that because I was confronting him. Jacob has never confronted Mason, but that hasn't stopped him from ending up in hospital. At what point does Mason take some responsibility for his actions?'

'These are all things that the youth court will determine,' the policeman tells us before excusing himself, though surely only because this conversation is getting very difficult.

But after watching him go, Guy and I share a nervous glance, and we're nervous because it sounds like all it might take for Mason to wriggle his way out of this mess is to say that he has witnessed a few bad things in his childhood, and that he only acted out because he lacked a decent role model. While that might be enough to land his parents in trouble with the police, it might see Mason go unpunished, and that is not something I can stomach because that will not ensure Jacob's safety. If Mason isn't forced into changing his ways after this latest incident, where will it end?

I get proof that Guy is still just as concerned about that as I am a moment later when out of nowhere, he lashes out at the nearest wall, punching it as hard as he can before crying out in pain and looking down at his swollen, bloody and potentially broken knuckles.

As I stand here in a hospital corridor and watch my husband cradle his damaged hand, while I wait for news on my son's recovery, I can't help but wonder how my life has come to this.

I also can't help but fear that this is still only the tip of the iceberg.

TWENTY-TWO

GUY

If you're going to potentially fracture a bone in your hand, it's best to do it at a hospital where you can seek immediate medical attention.

As I sit on the edge of a bed and watch a nurse tending to my injured knuckles, I think about how this serves me right for doing something so stupid as punching a concrete wall. But I couldn't help it. I saw red and just lashed out at the nearest inanimate object, and my reason for losing my temper is my fear that Mason Burton will get away with yet another heinous act against an innocent person.

All that talk of the youth court and the various factors that will be considered might have been technically correct, but the more I heard about them, the more it sounded to me like numerous potential ways for a lawyer to get the suspect out of this. It's not hard to imagine a legal professional spinning a few lines to a judge about how Mason has had a challenging upbringing and that, coupled with his age and whatever 'remorse' he pretends to show for the court, might just be enough to see him walk out of there with nothing more than a slap on the wrist.

While I feel sympathy for anybody who has had a troubled upbringing, because it's not their fault what type of home they are born into, that sympathy is stretched to its limits when the sake of my own child's wellbeing is at stake. That's why it would be extremely worrying if a judge did allow Mason to go unpunished, not least because hiding in the bushes and attacking Jacob showed a level of premeditation that a spontaneous crime lacks, but also because just like all the other things that boy has done in the past, he is guilty as sin. I know it, Sara knows it, Jacob sure does, as does the Atkinson family and most likely half the police officers in this town. But, unfortunately, the only person that matters is the judge in that court, and whatever they decide will be upheld.

Despite doing my best to think positively, I can't help but predict that this will not have a satisfactory ending for anybody other than the person who did wrong here. That prediction is why I punched the wall and, therefore, why I am now being treated as a patient in this hospital alongside my son. But my injuries are all of my own doing. After I have been tended to I leave the nurse with a heavily bandaged hand and a bruised ego, and return to the room where Jacob is recuperating.

I find Sara sitting by our son's bedside, watching over him as he sleeps. It's late now, nearly ten o'clock, but the nurses on this particular ward have told us that we don't have to abide by visiting times just yet. That's a relief, as much for them as it is for us, because I'm sure they wouldn't have liked to have to deal with my wife if they'd told her she had to go home when she wasn't ready to.

'Hey,' I say as I take a seat beside Sara and, as I do, I notice her wipe away a tear that had been silently rolling down her cheek.

'Hey. How's your hand?' she asks me, and I gingerly lift my injured limb to show her what a good job the nurse did of bandaging it.

'I'll survive,' I say before apologising for giving Sara something else to worry about on top of all this.

'I just want this to end,' she tells me as another tear escapes her eye and, despite our difficulties lately, it breaks my heart to see her this upset.

I wipe away her tear, using my good hand to soak it up before I kiss Sara's forehead and tell her that everything will be okay. The problem is that it feels mighty hard to believe that when we're sitting only a few centimetres away from where our son is lying in bed, his head wrapped in bandages and his arm hooked up to an IV drip so that he can get some fluids into him.

'Oh gosh, we haven't even told Amber yet,' Sara suddenly realises, and while I had actually considered our daughter before now, I had decided that there was no point worrying her at university until we knew that Jacob was going to be okay.

'I'll phone her in the morning,' I say, not looking forward to having such a difficult conversation but knowing it needs to be done at some point. One thing our daughter requested of us before leaving to go to uni was that she be kept abreast of any news in the family, clearly afraid that being out of sight might mean she was also out of the loop when it came to the goings-on at home. Well, this certainly qualifies as news, though not of the good variety.

'You should go back to the house and get some rest,' Sara suggests, making it clear she is happy for me to leave my chair at the bedside, but also clear that she has no plans to leave hers.

'No way, I'm not leaving you. I want to be here.'

'I'll be fine. And Jacob will sleep all night. They're going to give him some pretty strong painkillers, so he'll be out for a while soon.'

'It's okay, I'll stay here with you.'

'No, please. Go home and get some rest. There's no point in both of us being exhausted. One of us needs to be alert in case the police need to talk to us again.'

I spend a few more minutes trying to get Sara to drop it, but in the end I accept her wish for me to leave. Just before I go Jacob wakes up from his latest nap.

He's groggy as well as thirsty, the latter issue we can deal with relatively quickly by handing him a plastic cup of water. After dealing with his dry throat, when he puts the cup down, I see a very melancholy expression on his face. However, it doesn't seem like there is much point in either me or Sara asking him what is wrong, because it's blatantly obvious as he lies here in hospital with numerous injuries on his body. But it's actually far worse than that and we get confirmation when Jacob speaks quietly.

'I'm scared of seeing Mason again,' he says meekly with tears in his eyes. But then he goes even further. 'I can't see him again. I just can't.'

While it's obvious why Jacob would not wish to cross paths with his tormentor ever again, it's the way that my son just said it that frightens me. It wasn't so much him voicing a fear as him voicing a fact. He can't see Mason again. But with no guarantee of Mason ever leaving him alone, how could he be sure he'd never see him again?

Unless he did something drastic.

Unless he did what Zoe Atkinson did.

'Hey, come on, buddy, everything's going to be okay,' I say as an awful feeling rises up inside of me. 'You don't have to worry about Mason any more.'

But as things stand, that is a lie and Jacob knows it as well as I do. That's why he just rolls over and closes his eyes and ends this conversation right there. But he's already said enough and both Sara and I know it, though it remains unspoken between us, because voicing our biggest fear isn't something we're quite ready to do at this time. Instead, I just carry on with the plan before Jacob woke up, which involves me going home to get some rest.

After giving both her and my resting son a kiss on the head, I make my way out of the hospital, my thoughts a blur and the knot in my stomach as tight as it has ever been since this whole ordeal started.

The drive home is tricky with only one good hand but I manage it, in no small part due to the fact that I turned down any pain-relief medication, meaning that while my body is hurting, my mind is clear enough for me to navigate these roads safely. But getting home is one thing; achieving any kind of meaningful rest is quite another. While I do drop off occasionally, sunrise comes about, and I'd say I managed less than three hours sleep in total in the end.

It's still far too early in the day to call Amber with the news about her brother, so I spend my last bit of time at home packing up a change of clothes for Sara, as well as a few snacks that will make her bedside vigil at the hospital a little easier when I get back to her. Then I go to leave, but once I'm back in my car, I think of somewhere else I want to go before I get back to the hospital.

It's a place I spent plenty of time thinking about last night while I lay in bed, staring up at the ceiling with my injured hand on my chest, and, as I drive, I decide I am definitely going to go there now. I only slow down when Mason's home comes into view, and as I park up a little way down the street, I decide that this time, my visit here will be different. I'm not going to go and bang on the front door before getting into a fistfight with Dean Burton, nor am I going to do anything that might end up being captured on video by Mason himself. And staying away from Tracey, that gobby cow, is probably a good idea too. Instead, what I am going to do is watch, and as I sit there on the quiet street, the clock on my dashboard telling me it's approaching half past eight in the morning, I realise what I am doing.

I'm being clever.

It's become obvious that getting angry and going in all guns blazing is not the right strategy when it comes to dealing with the Burtons. They can give as good as they get, if not more, and for all I know, they have had plenty of practice in dealing with angry parents of other children and most likely the police too. Therefore, I need to come up with a different approach, and as I see the front door of the Burton house open, I am set on what that will be.

I'm going to watch them. I'm going to learn their routines. Their routes. Their habits. And then, once I have that information, I can decide whether or not I'm going to use it against them.

As I watch Mason Burton leave his house in a school uniform that I recognise as belonging to St Anne's, the school on Smithson Lane, and obviously the school that Mason is now attending after being kicked out of his previous two, I think about how this boy's fate should lie in the hands of a judge in a youth court.

I say *should* because it doesn't have to.

Mason Burton's fate could lie in the hands of somebody else, I suppose.

My hands.

What if I was to intervene? Dole out a little justice of my own? Do what somebody in this town should have done a long time ago and put an end to this boy's reign of terror?

Would I? Is it possible? And most importantly, could I get away with it?

As I watch Mason Burton walk alone down the street in the direction of his new school, I consider all the possible options and outcomes.

But the fact I haven't made my mind up by the time I return to the hospital to see Jacob again, tells me that, at present, no option is currently off the table.

TWENTY-THREE

SARA

It's been a long night at the hospital, made much longer by me only having this uncomfortable chair to try and sleep in. But the main thing is that I was here whenever Jacob woke up and needed to see a familiar face to give him a little comfort in this rather disturbing environment.

He did wake a couple of times, the first time around 2 a.m., and when he did, he complained of being in pain. Fortunately, a nurse was on hand to administer him some more relief, and he drifted off again not long after that. But he woke once more before dawn, and despite saying the same thing to the nurse regarding his pain levels, she was unable to offer him anything else until a little more time had passed. That meant Jacob was unable to get back to sleep, grimacing and groaning as he shuffled in the bed and tried to get comfortable, all the while with me sat beside him offering him a few comforting words, but little in the way of anything that could actually make a difference to his pain.

By far and away, the worst point came when the nurses arrived to give Jacob his breakfast. That was because despite my son saying he was hungry, it was still not possible for him to eat solid foods with his broken teeth and swollen jaw. The best they could do was put another drip in him, more wires coming out of the bruised arms of my boy, and when Jacob started to cry just before 8 a.m., I wished there was something I could do to help him.

I felt so powerless, and I'm still feeling that way now as Guy arrives carrying a rucksack that he tells me contains a few items of clothing and some toiletries to help me freshen up, as well as a magazine, sweets and a couple of bottles of water. But I feel bad eating the sweets in front of Jacob when he can't eat them himself, just as I feel bad about showering and getting changed when he can barely manage sitting up in bed, which is why I don't open the rucksack even when Guy suggests I do so for a third time.

'Leave it,' I say to him to let him know he's not to keep pestering me, certainly not after a night without sleep, and he does just that, going quiet and staring out of the window that overlooks yet another dreary-looking building that makes up this hospital complex.

I ask Guy if he managed to get any rest at home, and he tells me that he did, although the dark circles under his eyes suggest he might be telling me a white lie there.

'What else did you do?' I ask him, making conversation if only to pass another minute or so in this awful room.

'Not much. Just slept, had a piece of toast and then came back here,' he tells me, and I have no reason not to believe him. I do wonder, though, if he might have opened a bottle of something strong last night when he got back, a little something to take the edge off the pain he is feeling over his son being hurt. But I won't pry. I'm sure he did whatever he felt he needed to do.

I just wish I could have done what I felt I needed to do too.

It was during my long night in this chair that I found myself unable to think of anything else but getting revenge on

Mason Burton and his family. Every time I looked at my son's swollen face, I quickly thought of Mason's and how I'd love to wipe the smile off it, given half the chance. Each occasion I heard Jacob let out a moan of discomfort, I thought about how I'd like to make Mason cry out in pain, too, if only a little bit. And when Jacob began crying earlier, tears streaming down his horribly bruised cheeks, I dreamt about getting my revenge on the Burton family, because life isn't fair in its current state.

But that's all it has been so far. Dreams. Fantasies. Wishes. In other words, all things that are as useless as the police have been in getting justice for both Jacob and the late Zoe.

I've also spent a lot of time thinking about Mason's parents and what they might have been doing while I was stuck here in this hospital worried sick about my son. They would have been at home, sat around the TV, laughing at whatever they were watching, while eating and drinking to their hearts' content, with no such worries on their minds because life always seems to work out okay for the Burtons.

I hate that family with such a strong feeling that it frightens me. But as I watch Jacob struggle once more to do something as simple as scratch an itch on his arm, I feel the anger washing over me again. That anger only intensifies after Guy has gone outside to phone Amber and let her know what's going on with her brother – a difficult conversation to have and one that leaves him looking utterly drained when he returns to the room.

'Your sister is going to drive home so she can see you,' Guy tells Jacob once he's retaken his seat beside the bed, and while our son is annoyed that he is now interfering with his sister's enjoyment of university, I'm sure he is excited to see his sibling again. I feel like it will be nice to have the four of us back together, if only for a short while. But, in the meantime, my anger continues to bubble beneath the surface, and just like a volcano it can't go on bubbling quietly forever. Eventually, there has to be an eruption and, when it comes, it promises to be destructive.

For me, that eruption threatens to break through to the surface when Jacob sees us looking forlorn by his bed and tells us that this isn't our fault.

'I just wish there was a way to make Mason go away,' he tells us as I try not to focus too much on the loose tooth that becomes visible when he speaks. 'He will go to prison for this, won't he?'

Guy and I share a look before we tell our son what he wants to hear. Being forced to tell him what might be a lie is the final straw for me, and I decide I've had enough and storm out of the room, unable to control my emotions any longer.

Eruption?

Check.

Guy chases me out into the corridor, and I know I should go back in the room soon, if only to stop Jacob worrying about me, but for the time being, I need to stay out here, away from the blood, bruises and bleeping machines.

'What is it? What's wrong?' Guy asks me, concern all over his face.

'What's wrong? I'll tell you what's wrong! Our son is in there in agony, and the boy who put him in here is out there getting on with his life!'

'I know, but what do you want me to do about it? We've spoken to the police.'

'And you think that'll make a difference?'

'I didn't say that. But what else can we do?'

'I don't know! But I have to do something. I feel like I'm going mad here!'

I expect Guy to put his arms around me and say a few reassuring words before leading me back into Jacob's room, and trying to persuade me that a shower and change of clothes will make me feel better. But he doesn't do that. Instead, he gets as honest as I am.

'I went to Mason's house this morning,' he says, much to my surprise.

'You did what?'

'I know, it was a stupid idea. But I just found myself driving there, and when I got there, I saw him. Mason. He was going to school. He's at St Anne's now. You were right, he's out there getting on with his life while Jacob is in here, and it isn't fair.'

'So what are you suggesting?'

'I don't know. All I do know is that when I was watching him, it took all my restraint not to put my foot on the accelerator and drive straight into him.'

'Guy!'

'What?'

'Please don't say something like that again!'

'Why not? I want to make sure that Mason never hurts our son again. Don't you?'

'Yes, of course I do, but we can't do anything stupid. Jacob needs us. What good would it do if we were in prison?'

'What if we could do something without getting caught?'

I stare at my husband and process his question. While I thought he had come out into this corridor to try and calm me down, it seems now that he might have just been waiting for me to crack before seizing the opportunity to suggest something that has clearly been brewing in his mind overnight.

'What do you mean?' I ask him, nervous but curious at the same time.

'I don't know,' Guy admits, running a hand over his tired face before fixing me with an intense stare. 'But this goes beyond being about Jacob, even though that's obviously my biggest priority. I want to ensure Mason can't hurt anyone's child ever again, but, based on his history, I'd say it's unlikely he'll avoid bullying someone else in future. I'm not sure I could live with myself if I stood by and did nothing and then found out someone else had been hurt or killed themselves after what he had done to them.'

Guy looks as if he's wondering if I will tell him to not think about it like that, and try to persuade him that not only will Jacob be okay but everyone else who encounters Mason in the future will be too. But I don't. Instead, I reluctantly admit I feel exactly the same way.

And that was it. That was the moment the pair of us crossed a line that would change our lives and the lives of several other people forever. Of course, we didn't quite realise the significance of the moment at that time. We were just two stressed, angry and sleep-deprived parents standing in a hospital corridor, trying not to be overheard by any nurses and preparing to put on a brave face again for our son.

But that was when we did it.

That was when we truly decided that we were going to get revenge.

NOW

TWENTY-FOUR

GUY

It's been thirteen days since Mason first attacked Jacob. It's been four days since Jacob was admitted to hospital after the second, more vicious beating. And it's been three days since Sara and I decided that enough was enough.

Since then, the pair of us have been extremely busy planning, or to give it its proper name, *plotting*.

Consumed by a toxic combination of anger towards Mason, a lack of trust in the justice system and an unhealthy dose of guilt about failing to keep our son safe, my wife and I are taking matters into our own hands. We're gaining back some measure of control; control that we lost when Jacob came home covered in blood, and control that has to be better than sitting powerlessly by a hospital bed and waiting for the scars to heal.

Sara has mostly been by that hospital bed over the last three days, keeping an eye on Jacob as he slowly but surely recovered, getting a little bit better, now able to eat somewhat more normally, as well as go to the toilet without breaking down in tears because his head hurts so much. But I spent less time at the hospital over the last seventy-two hours than my wife did, and the reason for that is I've been ramping up my surveillance of the Burtons. So much so that I know exactly where Mason goes and at what time, down to the exact street at the exact second.

Mason leaves his house at 8:35 a.m. every day and sets off on foot by himself in the direction of St Anne's school, his new place of education and the latest establishment to take a chance on 'reforming' the troubled teen. It's a twenty-minute walk to school for Mason, and he doesn't seem to have the option of getting a lift from his parents, nor do they put him on a bus. He just leaves home and walks, whatever the weather, and when he does, he always follows the same route.

Left out of his street. Down Catterall Close, then right onto Fern Crescent. From there, he crosses the main road at Dean Junction and heads into the industrial estate known as Little Fulton. It might sound quaint but it's a rough part of town, not that a boy like Mason has much to worry about, swaggering through the streets with not the slightest care in the world. I even observed him pausing outside a house one morning before sneaking into the front garden, stealing a newspaper that was poking out of a letterbox, and then tossing it into the next-door neighbour's bin. There was no reason for him to do such a thing other than sheer petulance, and it was yet another example of what a 'lovely' boy he is.

It takes twelve minutes for him to get through the estate, before he completes his journey by crossing two more streets and finally walking through the school gates at St Anne's, where he spends the day most likely terrorising a whole new batch of pupils that he previously did not have access to before he got expelled from his last school.

After studying Mason's journey to his new school, it's the part just after the estate that interests me the most, because that's the only part of the route where he passes down a section of street that is not overlooked by any houses. It's a stretch of road flanked by two high walls overlooking a disused railway

line, and when Mason is there, he's the only one around. Or at
least he thought he was, but if he had only looked back over his
shoulder, then he would have seen me following him on foot
over the last three days.

Having witnessed him making that walk to school, I ascer-
tained the best place for me to intercept him on that route, and
once I'd done that, I could share that information with Sara. It
was during another sleep-deprived day when I enlightened her
about what I'd learnt following Mason and, once I had, she
wanted to act quickly, mainly because delaying any longer
would put us both at risk of chickening out and deciding not to
act after all.

But today is the day.

We are actually doing this.

Jacob was allowed home yesterday to continue his recovery
in more pleasant surroundings and, now that he is, Sara and I
don't have to keep up appearances at the hospital. Amber being
back home gives us an extra pair of hands to help out with the
patient. So there is a window of time when Sara and I can leave
the house and go out to do what we need to do.

*And that window of time began at eight thirty-five this
morning when Mason left his house to walk to school.*

I check my watch and see that it is 8:50 a.m., and that tells
me Mason should almost be through the estate now, and be
about to pass along this stretch of road by the high walls. It's
beside one of those walls that I am lurking now, on a slight bend
in the road, out of view of any approaching pedestrians, and I've
been here since Sara dropped me off just before sunrise. I
wanted to get here by car, so nobody would report seeing a man
matching my description on foot in this estate around the time
Mason went missing.

It's been a tedious wait for me as I've stood here and
counted down the minutes, but as well as being confident that
nobody has seen me around this morning, I have enjoyed visual-

ising all the things I'm going to say and do to Mason when I've finally got my hands on him. It's about time I got the chance to right so many of the wrongs he has committed. But, just to be sure that no one will see and identify me, Mason included, I am wearing a hat, dark glasses and sporting a small beard from not having shaved for a few days, which belies my usually clean-shaven appearance. And now, as another minute passes, I finally leave my hiding place and begin walking down the street, though I'm not going in the direction of the school this time.

I'm going the opposite way.

The way in which Mason will be approaching me.

I keep my head down and my pace steady as I walk, and I only look up briefly when I hear the sound of whistling up ahead. It's him. I recognise the school uniform, the confident gait, but most of all I recognise the smug look on the boy's face.

Mason continues to whistle as he gets nearer, and if he was really switched on, then he might think about how this is the first time he's ever crossed paths with somebody on this part of his journey. But he's not observant. As he gets closer, I take a deep breath and keep my head down. But I'm not just trying to keep my identity a secret until the last second, I'm also listening out for the sound of a car engine, because when I hear it I'll have to act fast.

And there it is.

I look up to see a very recognisable car turning onto the street behind Mason, and there is my wife, sitting behind the wheel and staring right at me through the windscreen. I turn my attention away from her and look right at Mason, and just before he can make eye contact with me I make my move.

Lunging forward and grabbing the burly youngster by the arms, I catch him completely off guard, and it takes him a second to even start fighting back. But it doesn't matter when he does because not only do I have a firm grip on him, I don't need to hold on to him for long. That's because Sara races up and parks right beside us before getting out and opening the boot of the car.

'Get off me! What are you doing?' Mason cries out before I bundle him into the back of the car and slam the lid shut, trapping him inside, in a place where his next noises are extremely muffled. Sara is already back behind the wheel, so I run around to sit beside her in the passenger seat, and once my door is closed she hits the accelerator pedal, getting us out of there as quickly as possible.

Reminding her to slow down and follow the speed limit once we reach the more populated main road again, she does as I ask, and we fall in with the rest of the early morning traffic, stopping at red lights, starting again at green ones and generally looking just like any other car out on the road. But, of course, that's not what we are, because I suspect we're the only car out this morning with a person trapped in the boot.

But that person won't be in there for long, and as we turn off the main road and begin making our way out of town, I think about what will happen when I let Mason back out into daylight.

He'll be relieved to see the sky and breathe fresh air again, no doubt.

Unfortunately for him, it'll only be the beginning of what is to come.

TWENTY-FIVE

SARA

We've done it. We've got Mason.

And there is no going back now.

I know all the reasons I had that led me to this decisive and dramatic course of action, but that doesn't mean it's any easier now that I'm in the middle of it. At least my husband seems to be holding it together so far, or perhaps he's just a little better than me when it comes to acting like everything is okay.

But things are definitely not okay.

'I can't believe we've done this! What were we thinking?' I cry as I put my hands on my head and keep pacing around outside the abandoned warehouse in the countryside that Guy identified as being the ideal place for us to bring our prisoner once we'd captured him.

'Calm down! This is what we discussed,' Guy says, doing a lot less pacing but still moving around a fair bit himself, a sure sign that he possesses plenty of nervous energy too. 'Everything has gone to plan so far, so there is nothing to worry about.'

'Nothing to worry about? We have a violent young offender tied up in that warehouse!' I say, jabbing a finger towards the derelict building that is the only thing out here on this other-wise desolate and disused wasteland of grass and rubble.

'You wanted to do this just as much as I did,' Guy reminds me, though I sure am glad there are no police officers around to hear him when he says it. 'Don't bail out on me now. I need you to help me see this through.'

I feel sick when our plot is put into such basic, sterile terms as 'see this through', and before I know it I'm bent over double, my hands on my knees, and it's physically all I can do to stop myself from retching.

'Sara! Get it together! We don't have time for this!'

Guy grabs one of my hands and pulls me towards him, forcing me to stand upright again. Once I am he puts both his hands on my shoulders and looks me squarely in the eyes.

'Just breathe! Take deep breaths. Come on now, Sara, we've come this far we can't lose it now. Think of Jacob. And Amber. They'll need us to make it back home safely. And think of Zoe and her family. What they lost because of that menace in there. This is for them too. We're righting a wrong here today. We're ridding the world of a bad person, a person who will surely hurt many more people if he's left to his own devices. Okay?'

Guy didn't need to give me the little pep talk because he's not saying anything that he hasn't said before or anything that I haven't thought before either. But hearing it one more time does go some way to snapping me out of my trance and pulling me back into the moment. Once I'm in the right mental state again, I start to calm down and realise that he is right. Revenge, ridding the world of bad, righting wrongs, all of that is true. But most of all, it's what he said about Jacob and Amber and how they need us to come home and not go to prison. And that is why I have come to my conclusion.

'We are not doing this,' I say to Guy firmly. 'We are not killing Mason Burton.'

Guy hears what I have to say before taking his hands off my

shoulders, and he trudges away from me, looking like he's now the one in a daze, before he reaches the side of the warehouse and slides his back down it, taking a seat on the ground and hanging his head. The knife he planned to use on Mason is currently lying on the floor in the warehouse after he threw it down to the ground in frustration upon realising it was going to be much harder to use than first anticipated.

'You're right,' he admits after a couple of quiet moments in which the only sound existing between us is the swirling of the wind out in this exposed area. 'We're not killers. I can't believe I ever thought we could actually do this.'

'We were just angry,' I say as I go over and take a seat beside him, my back now pressing into the cold, hard exterior of the warehouse. 'And shocked. And scared. We weren't in our right minds after seeing our son covered in blood and needing hospital treatment. Any parent could sympathise with that. But the main thing is that we've come to our senses now before it's too late.'

As I sit there, my mind rushes through the plot we made, and I'm terrified at how close we came to actually carrying it all out.

Guy did a good job of tracking Mason's movements to the point where we were easily able to abduct the boy on a quiet street at the exact time we predicted without any witnesses around. My hands had been drenched in sweat as I had driven our car to the agreed meeting point, and my heart had been thumping in my chest when I had helped Guy bundle Mason into the boot. After that, the plan had called for me to drive us all here to this warehouse, where we would then tie up Mason with the rope Guy had picked up from a DIY store yesterday. And then, once we had told Mason exactly why we were doing this and let him know that he had brought this all on himself, Guy was to use a knife to end Mason's life, thus ensuring that not only Jacob was safe from him in the future, but any other parents' kids were safe too.

It all seemed so simple, and for the most part, it worked. Right up until the part where we actually have to do the stabbing. Guy had even raised the knife above his head in preparation to end this once and for all as Mason cowered beneath him, looking up at us with frightened eyes. But just before Guy could bring the knife down, I had started to freak out and I'd run outside the warehouse to get some air. Guy had followed me, and we've been out here ever since, debating, deciding, but most of all, dithering.

'There's just one problem if we let him go,' Guy says as the wind continues to whip around the decrepit building behind us. 'Mason has seen our faces. He knows we are the ones who abducted him. All he has to do is tell somebody, and we're in big trouble.'

That is quite the problem, but as I think about it, I see a possible way out.

'You're looking at this all wrong,' I say, hoping I'm right as I speak. 'Mason won't be angry at us, not after we've made it clear we could have easily killed him. If we do let him go, he'll be so grateful to be alive that he won't speak about this to anyone. And we can make sure he agrees to that before we untie him.'

'And you'd take his word for it, would you? That he wouldn't tell anyone?'

'We'd have to. What else can we do?'

'I don't know!'

Maybe this isn't as simple as I want it to be. It's one thing to decide not to kill somebody but it's another to just untie them, tell them to go and, best of all, just forget it ever happened.

No harm done. Carry on with your life. As you were.

Yeah, right.

As much as I desperately want to believe that Mason won't

tell anybody about this, I know as well as Guy does that we cannot take that risk.

'I knew we should have worn balaclavas,' I say, referring to the point in our plotting where I suggested to my husband that we disguise ourselves more significantly.

'And you know what I said to that? It wouldn't have looked strange with you driving around town with a balaclava on your head, would it? And how the hell would Mason ever get close enough for me to grab him if I had a balaclava over my head? He'd have seen me and gone running in the opposite direction!'

'But now he knows it's us, what can we do?' I cry as a few raindrops begin to fall from the darkening sky overhead, a sky that makes this grim, abandoned place feel even more desperate than it already is.

'I have no idea,' Guy replies, brushing a few raindrops off the sleeve of his jacket, though it's a pointless act because there are plenty more drops to take their place. 'But we better decide soon. We've already taken too long. We need to get home, and Mason will be missing from school now. His parents might have been called, and people could already be looking for him.'

Guy's right, we need to make a decision, and we need to make it fast, so I get to my feet, and he does the same.

'Let's go and talk to him,' I suggest as the rain gets harder. 'Maybe if we can convey just how upset and angry we were over what he did to Jacob, he might understand. If that doesn't work, we'll just have to threaten him. Tell him that we'll let him go, but if he breathes a word of this to anyone, then we'll kill not only him but the rest of his family too.'

'Jesus, Sara, you're beginning to frighten me now.'

'As long as I frighten Mason, then that's all we need.'

With that, I head for one of the several open doorways that create voids around the four sides of this empty, cavernous warehouse and, once I'm in, my footsteps begin to echo as I move over the concrete floor.

Mason is on the far side of this warehouse, in a small room at the back of the disused property, and Guy and I quickly make our way back to him, preparing ourselves to enter the room and see our prisoner just as we left him, bound and gagged and with a whole lot of fear in his eyes.

But we don't find Mason how we left him at all.

We find him in a much worse state than he was earlier.

As we enter the room, I scream, while Guy puts his hands to his mouth and tries not to gag. That's because Mason Burton has ended up getting what's coming to him.

He's dead, and he has a large incision across his throat and blood all over his chest to prove it.

Someone has snuck in here and slit his throat while we were outside, presumably coming through one of the other open doors around the building. I don't know who they are, but I do know one thing. *They used my knife to do this.*

I know that because I can see it lying on the ground and while it was clean when Guy left it, it is now covered in blood.

Someone finished what we were supposed to have started.

But who?

And where the hell are they now?

TWENTY-SIX

GUY

I'm staring at Mason Burton, or the late Mason Burton as he should now be known, and all I can think about is how is this possible?

We brought him here to kill him.

So how could somebody beat us to it?

It's not hard to tear my eyes away from the sight of all the blood leaking out of the teenager, and as I look around the warehouse, I'm on guard in case whoever killed Mason is still here and might come after me or Sara next. But I can't see anybody and neither can my wife.

But that doesn't mean we're safe.

'We need to get out of here,' I say quietly. But she pulls away from me and doesn't move from her spot, just staring at Mason and what has become of him.

'Sara! We need to go! Whoever did this might still be here!'

I keep my voice as hushed as I can, afraid that the killer might overhear me if they are still lurking somewhere inside this huge warehouse, that's a terrifying thought.

'Sara, come on!' I say, tugging on my wife's hand and trying to snap her out of her trance.

'We did this,' she says, pulling away from me and looking like she's mad with me, as if I was the one who slit this boy's throat and not anybody else.

'What are you talking about?'

'It's our fault he's dead! We brought him here! We tied him up! He was defenceless because of us!'

'But we didn't kill him! Somebody else did that!'

'But who?'

'I have no idea, but I don't want to hang around here to try and find out. I just want to get you home and fast!'

'But what about the body? We can't just leave it here.'

'What else can we do? We can't report it, or the police will think we killed him. We have a motive, remember!'

'But it's not right to leave him. Look at him!'

Sara points at the body behind me, but I don't turn around because I don't need to see it again.

'Mason is dead, and nothing is going to change that. All we can do is make this situation worse for ourselves. We have to get out of here, and then we have to act as if nothing has happened.'

'Like nothing has happened? We kidnapped Mason and now he's dead!'

'We don't have time for this. We're not safe here!'

I give up trying to be gentle with my wife and pull her towards me, shaking her, so she comes to her senses.

'Sara! Think of the kids! We have to go! Now!'

That seems to do the trick, and as I set off towards the door, she follows closely behind me.

Then I remember something, and it was part of the original plan before everything went crazy. If we were to have killed Mason, I was going to remove the ropes from around his wrists and ankles, just in case they could be traced back to me when I bought them.

I would also have taken the knife.

Turning back to the body, I tell myself that I should still

remove the ropes, even though I'm not actually the killer here, so I step closer to the body. Trying not to get any blood on me, which is an almost impossible task, I start to remove the ropes.

'What are you doing?' Sara cries, looking as horrified as I feel.

'We need to get rid of this rope. It could be traced back to me buying it,' I say.

'Get away from him!'

'It'll just take a second.'

It ends up taking a little longer than that, but it's not easy trying to do a task like this, and it's made worse with all the adrenaline coursing around my body. I feel wired like my head is spinning and my heart is going to leap out of my chest and run away across this warehouse floor, but I have to hold it together just long enough to get this over with.

As all the ropes come free, I wrap them up into a small bundle, and I know that's one crucial piece of evidence taken care of. But the second piece won't be so easy to deal with.

Staring at the knife with the crimson-coloured blade, I wish I could just leave it be, but I know it could be traced back to me. The last thing I need is an investigating officer looking into me as a suspect and then realising there is one knife missing from the set in my kitchen, and that missing item just so happens to be the same size and model as the murder weapon found at the scene.

Grimacing as I bend down, I tentatively grab the knife by the handle that is thankfully clean of blood before taking that with me too.

'Come on!' I say, running back to the door, and Sara doesn't argue again.

I pause as I reach the doorway, peering through it to see if anybody might be lurking on the other side, but the warehouse looks clear, so we start running again, and once we get outside, it's a relief to be in the fresh air. But I make sure to keep my head on a swivel, looking left and right as we rush back to the car, because the killer could still be around somewhere, preparing to pounce from many of the open doors around this empty shell of a structure.

But I've not seen another person by the time we get back to our vehicle, and as I get in behind the wheel and Sara jumps into the passenger seat, I think we are going to get out of here, not that it will mean this is over.

Far from it.

I start the engine and spin the car around, the tyres churning up bits of rubble on the makeshift track that leads to this abandoned place, and once the car is heading away from the crime scene, I look back at it in my rear-view mirror. But I still don't see anybody else out here. No other cars. No one running away. No clue as to who might have been out here with me, Sara and Mason. But somebody has been, and that means that somebody will know what we were going to do.

'What do we do when the police find the body?' Sara asks me as I keep my foot on the accelerator.

'I don't know. Hopefully, they won't find it for a while. It could be weeks before anybody comes out here, maybe longer. We might get lucky.'

'Lucky? What part of this would you call lucky?'

'We wanted Mason dead and now he is. But we didn't have to do it, somebody else did. I guess he had other enemies.'

'That doesn't mean we're innocent!'

'No, but it means whoever did kill him has just as much to lose as us, if not more, so why would they tell anyone about this? If we all just keep it a secret, then everything will be okay.'

'God, I wish I had your optimism,' Sara says, shaking her head as I eventually bring us back towards the main road.

I make sure to keep the car well back from the road until I am sure that there are no other vehicles passing at this point and when there aren't, I pull out and put my foot down again.

'We just need to go home and act normal,' I tell Sara. 'Just like we were going to do if we had killed Mason ourselves.'

'You think we can do that? Because I don't!'

'We don't have any choice, Sara! We have to do it, or we're going to prison for the rest of our lives, and Jacob and Amber will be by themselves!'

We spend the majority of the rest of the journey in silence, a journey that ends up taking far longer than either of us would like, because we encounter a set of temporary traffic lights caused by some road maintenance going on a couple of miles from our house.

'What did you go this way for?' Sara asks me, having noticed that I altered my route home slightly.

'I'm just zigzagging around town a little,' I reply, thinking it makes sense to do such a thing, because if any police officer was ever to suspect us and look for our car on CCTV, then they'd see us in all sorts of different places this morning, and that has to be better than just seeing us making a direct route from the warehouse to home.

After a long-winded journey designed to confuse any police officer who might look into it, I've never been so happy to see my house by the time I turn the car onto our street and park on our driveway beside Amber's car. But just before we go inside, I give Sara one more pep talk.

'We can do this. We can be okay. We just need to keep calm and remember that everything is fine now. Jacob won't be having any more trouble with Mason Burton, and that's ulti-mately what we wanted to ensure, right?'

Sara says nothing, just stares through the windscreen at the house where our two children currently reside. Peaceful. Safe.

Innocent.

Unlike their parents.

'Sara?'

'Okay,' she mumbles back before getting out, and as I follow suit I have to hope that she will be able to hold it together as much as I hope to do so myself. But while Sara unlocks the front door and goes inside, I have one more thing to take care of.

The ropes.

I need to dispose of them, and quickly.

Carrying them to the bin around the back of my house, I can't wait to get rid of them. The bins are due to be collected tomorrow, so that is perfect, but as I open the lid and prepare to stuff the ropes into one of the bin bags already inside, I pause because I spot something.

There's a small red mark on one of the ropes.

It's only when I look a little closer that I realise it is a drop of Mason's blood.

TWENTY-SEVEN

SARA

I'm a nervous wreck, rattling around the house like a lost ghost, unsure of anything, jumping at the slightest noise and overre-acting to even the smallest of stresses. Like when Amber dropped a teaspoon in the kitchen earlier. I almost leapt out of my skin before having to try and laugh it off and pretend like it was no big deal. But my daughter looked very confused as she left the kitchen before Guy had yet another quiet word with me and told me to try and calm down. But that was far easier said than done, and after informing my boss that I wasn't feeling well, I was able to avoid having to do any work from home, a task that was impossible in my current mental state. Guy seemed to manage it himself, though only because he said he wanted to keep up appearances and make it look like everything was normal at his end.

Figuring that it might be easier to get through the rest of this hellish day if I didn't have to see other people, I retreated to my bedroom, faking a migraine and telling the rest of my family that I needed to have a lie-down, and while that did help me avoid others, it also meant I ended up lying on the bed and replaying the crazy events of this morning in my head.

In the end, I got in the shower and stood under the water for several long minutes, taking deep breaths and trying to force the image of Mason's dead body out of my mind. It's for that same reason that I am dreading closing my eyes because I just know that I will see him whenever I do.

'How are you feeling?' the voice from the other side of my bedroom door asks an hour after I have got out of the shower and got back into bed again.

It's Jacob. As he pokes his bruised head around the door, I force a smile onto my face and pretend like everything is fine.

'I'm okay, love, how are you feeling?' I ask him, just as concerned about him and his condition as he obviously is about mine.

'Tired, but I'm all right,' he says before fully entering the room and perching on the edge of my bed in his dressing gown. I haven't seen him wearing anything but that dressing gown since he got home from hospital, but that's okay because he's still recovering from the ordeal he went through. His school has been great and told him to take as long as he needs, and I'll make sure that he doesn't go back to his normal routine until he has fully healed. But quite how long it will be until I can go back to my normal routine after what I've just been through is another question.

'Have you managed to get much sleep?' I ask my son as I make out several of the purple bruises on his face that are visible even though the curtains are shut in here.

'A bit,' he replies. 'Amber woke me up this morning when she went downstairs for breakfast.'

'She's always been heavy footed, that child,' I say, and we both laugh.

'I'm glad she's home, though.'

'Me too.'

Jacob goes quiet again then, but knowing him as well as I do, I know that means there is something on his mind, and while it takes a little coaxing, he eventually lets me know what is troubling him.

'I don't hate him because he's beaten me up,' he says quietly, his head bowed as if he's too ashamed to make eye contact with me. 'I hate him because I'm scared of him.'

I know exactly who Jacob is talking about, but, like my son, I can't bring myself to say his name, though for very different reasons.

'He's not going to hurt you any more,' I say before regretting it because I'm afraid I've already said too much.

'How do you know that? He can get to me anywhere. It doesn't matter that I won't see him at school any more. He could be at the park again or anywhere else.'

I realise that it's fine. Jacob didn't read anything into me saying that he won't see Mason again and just presumes I'm saying it to reassure him. But while my son is worried about ever crossing paths with that boy again, I know that is impossible now. The problem is, I can't put his mind at ease by telling him that.

'I promise you that he will leave you alone in future.'

'How do you know that?'

'Because the police have spoken to him, and he will get in even more trouble than he's already in if he goes anywhere near you again.'

I'm playing this right. I'm acting like everything is still the same, and Mason is under investigation by the police. Better that than acknowledging the truth: that he is dead in a warehouse on the other side of town.

'I just want things to go back to normal,' Jacob tells me, a small tear running down one of his many bruises. 'I hate all this. Not just what he did to me but how you and Dad have been worrying too.'

'Don't worry about us, love. We're always going to worry about you, whatever is going on. That's just the job of a parent.'

I sit up on the bed and put my arm around him, the sleeve of my dressing gown resting on the shoulders of his, and I'm glad to see that his tears seem to have stopped.

'We're going to put this all behind us,' I tell Jacob, though I'm talking to myself just as much as him. 'Just get yourself better, and everything will be okay, I promise.'

'Thanks, Mum,' Jacob says, and we share a hug before he says he's going to go downstairs and make himself something to eat.

'Get your father to make it for you. Or your sister. You're supposed to be resting.'

'Yes, Mum,' he says with a laugh as he leaves, and it's good to hear that sound again, even if I feel on the verge of tears a moment later when my bedroom door has closed, and I'm alone again.

Like Jacob, I just want all of this to be over with, but unlike him I know that it never will be. Even if Guy is right and we can stay quiet and somehow get away with what we did and what we know, it will never truly be over, will it? I'll always know what happened to Mason, even if the police don't. I'll know how he was abducted, how he ended up in that warehouse and, while I don't know who killed him, I know he ended up dead long before most other people in this town receive that information.

How can life ever be the same again because of that?

I have no idea how I manage it, but I eventually fall asleep, and when I wake up, it's late in the evening, and the rest of my family are getting ready for bed themselves. I force myself to get up and see each of them, giving hugs to my two children and squeezing them extra tightly, as if I fear the police coming through the door any moment and whisking me away, meaning I'll never get the chance to hug them again.

Guy comes into the bedroom once Amber and Jacob are in their rooms, and while we barely talk as he undresses and turns the light out, he does initiate a little conversation once he's beside me underneath the duvet.

'Today will be the hardest day, but we've got through it now,' he says to me very quietly so nobody in the house can hear us. 'I'm proud of you, and I love you. All we have to do now is stick together, and we'll be fine.'

I don't have the energy to argue with him, and Guy takes my silence as agreement, because he gives me a kiss before rolling over and trying to get some sleep of his own. But I'm wide awake after napping for most of the afternoon, so like many people who find themselves unable to sleep at night, I end up surfing the web on my mobile phone as I lie on my pillow. But I'm not just browsing the internet for anything. I'm looking at all the news websites, the local ones and the national ones, and I'm doing that because I need to check if there are any reports of a body being found at a warehouse in this town.

Thankfully, there are not, but I know it's only a matter of time until the headlines are full of the story of Mason Burton and the awful way in which his body was discovered. His parents must already know that he is missing and might have spoken to the police. A search could be underway for him already, and while that warehouse is very much off the beaten track, somebody is bound to go looking in there one day and, when they do, they will make a very grim discovery.

But until then, nobody knows what happened.

Nobody but me, my husband and whoever the actual killer is.

TWENTY-EIGHT

GUY

It's been two days since Sara and I fled the warehouse that holds Mason's body, and while every hour has been almost as excruciating as the last, there has still been no news. But it's not just the police I'm worried about hearing from at some point in the future.

I'm also concerned about Mason's killer making contact, whoever they may be.

They must have seen us and our car, meaning we're easily traceable if they wanted to get in touch. But would they? At present, they have got away with murder, so it would be advisable that they continue to maintain a low profile, not only now but for as long as they can. That would clearly be the best outcome for Sara and me too, but it remains to be seen whether or not that is what happens.

I'm sitting at the kitchen table trying to do some work, but I'm making slow progress on the report my boss has asked me to have completed by the start of next week. I obviously can't say anything to him, but menial auditing chores seem so insignificant when compared to things like dead bodies, police investigations and potential prison sentences. I guess I took having a clear conscience for granted throughout most of my life, but now that I can't get one of those back, I wish so much for a return to the days when I had nothing to worry about.

At least the ropes have gone now.

The bin bags were collected yesterday by the council and are no doubt already at the local dump, mixed in with every other resident's rubbish and untraceable back to me at this point. The knife I was going to use to kill Mason is back in the cutlery drawer only a few yards away from me after it had a very through clean, all traces of blood removed after several cycles through the dishwasher.

As much as I hope that the killer never tries to contact us, I also hope that they have been just as thorough with removing any evidence as I have been. The worst possible thing that could happen is that the police find the killer's DNA at the crime scene, track the culprit down and then, when they are being interrogated and desperately seeking some way to get a little leniency, they mention my name or Sara's. I need whoever this is to get away scot-free with their crime as much as I seem to have got away with mine, but only time will tell if that happens.

The house is quiet as I return to my work; the tapping of my fingers on my laptop's keyboard is the only sound in the house. Jacob is upstairs in his room, still sleeping most likely, while Sara is in the spare bedroom sitting at her workstation, a place I told her she had to be because it would start to look suspicious if she had any more time off work. She didn't like me saying that, but the fact that she hasn't been reporting for duty since we abducted Mason is not a good thing, and while I appreciate she is struggling to eat or sleep with all this on her mind, it's imperative that we all try to carry on as if nothing is wrong.

But the silence coming from the spare bedroom suggests she hasn't found it within herself to participate in any video calls with her colleagues yet, nor make any phone calls relating to her business. But hopefully she is doing something up there, even if it's just the bare minimum, like responding to a few simple emails. Anything that might make it look like all is well in her world, so that nobody can flag up any unusual actions should the police ever start asking any questions about our behaviour this week.

At least there's one member of my family who is carrying on as normal. Amber left late last night to drive back to university, satisfied that her brother was on the mend now and with a bellyful of home cooking to keep her going until the next time she is here. I wish she was still around because this house sure could do with her and her noisy ways, if only to break the awful silence that exists here and makes me want to shout out just to break it for a moment.

It's just before lunchtime when I find a perfectly valid reason to break that silence after all, because as I'm typing out an email to a colleague, my mobile phone beeps beside me, and when I look down at the screen, I see the news notification staring back at me.

Body found on disused land – Police begin murder investigation

The notification is from the local newspaper website, a site I've subscribed to for several years, though I've never paid too much attention to the news flashes that have popped up on my phone before. But then again, I've never been directly involved in any of the news stories before either, but that's all changed now. As I grab my phone, I hold my breath as I unlock my device and seek out further information on the troubling headline I just saw.

Unsurprisingly, the story is the top item on the website, but the article is only partially complete.

A dog walker made a grim discovery today when he discovered a body in the old ArcherMill warehouse on what was once the Kerrigan Industrial Estate. While the police have not yet released details about the identity of the deceased, it is believed that his family have been informed. At present, this is being treated as a murder investigation. More to follow...

I have to put my phone down before I'm sick all over it. This is it. Mason has been found and by a damn dog walker.

Why did they have to go inside the warehouse? Why couldn't they have just stayed away? If only they had, Mason might not have been found for ages. But the police know about him now and, according to the article, so do his parents.

I imagine Dean and Tracey and the shock they must have got when the police came to their door and informed them of what they had found. The pain. The tears. The anger. Their child is dead and they know it, and, somehow, despite wishing so many bad things on that family, as well as knowing how heartless they were when Zoe Atkinson died and her parents went through the same thing, I still find myself feeling sorry for them. But I'm feeling almost as sorry for myself, and that's because I know I better go and tell Sara about this before she comes across the news herself and gets as big a shock as I just did.

I slowly make my way up the stairs and towards the spare bedroom, dreading the conversation that I'm about to have but knowing it is a necessary one to get through. If I don't do this, then things could be so much worse. Sara might end up hearing the news when Jacob is with her and, if that happens, he will be sure to notice how badly his mother reacts to it, giving him serious cause for concern. I need to tell her in private, so we can process this together without anybody else around. Only then can we start to talk about this with other people, and when we do, we'll have to act just like them and say all the same sorts of things they will.

'Murder? I never thought anything like that could happen around here.'

'Who do you think did it?'

'Are our children safe?'

Those are just some of the sentiments and questions the residents of this town are likely to utter over the next few days, and as I push open the door to the spare bedroom, I see my wife sitting at her desk with her head in her hands. I wonder for a moment if she has already seen the news and is reacting to it, but she hasn't because she looks up at me, and after seeing my pale face, she asks me what is wrong.

So I tell her.

The police have a body.

The warehouse will currently be flooded with forensic experts.

And all we can do about it is hope that we are not a part of the next news headline.

TWENTY-NINE

SARA

I think I reacted better than Guy thought I would when he told me that the police had found the body. But that was only because I've gone into some kind of fugue state, and I'm still very much in that state when the next newsflash occurs.

Body found on Kerrigan Industrial Estate is local teenager, Mason Burton, 15.

That particular newsflash is rolling across the bottom of the TV screen as I sit and watch it in the living room with Guy and Jacob sitting on the opposite sofa. We've been gathered around the television since Guy made us our dinner, and despite knowing we should avoid it, my husband and I have been unable to tear ourselves away from watching the news.

Yes, the media always like to scaremonger, but in this case, what we are seeing and hearing is as frightening as it gets. And now Jacob thinks so too.

'Mason is dead?' he utters when he sees the familiar name appear on the screen, and it's only a moment later when the news reporter sitting behind the desk repeats the same name himself. 'What the hell happened?'

'I don't know,' Guy replies before looking at me, but I daren't say a word, and I'm thankful that the reporter on the screen is filling the silence for me.

'Mason Burton had been reported missing by his parents thirty-six hours ago. Their son had not attended his school, St Anne's, and while his absence initially was a case of suspected truancy, it became apparent something was wrong when he failed to return home at all during the rest of that day. The police began a search, but it was to have a tragic ending when a member of the public who was walking their dog on the disused Kerrigan estate made a grim discovery in the ArcherMill warehouse this morning. The cause of death is being treated as suspicious, and police are appealing for information from anybody who was in the area of the crime scene in the last forty-eight hours. More to follow after the break.'

The advertisements that start playing offer a welcome respite from the heavy subject being discussed, but while the news reporters have disappeared briefly, Jacob is only too quick to take up the mantle of discussing the topic further.

'They think somebody killed him?' he asks, his slowly healing face a picture of disbelief.

'It sounds like it,' Guy mumbles before fiddling awkwardly with the remote control. But he doesn't turn the television off, no matter how much he might want to.

'Who would do that? Who would kill him?'

Jacob's next questions go unanswered for a moment before Guy makes another quiet attempt at fielding them.

'You know what he was like,' he says to our son who is shaking his head in disbelief. 'He caused a lot of trouble. Got into a lot of fights. Maybe he messed with the wrong person.'

I really want Guy to shut up, but I guess that one of us has to talk to Jacob and rather him than me. But their conversation is stopped when we all hear the sound of car doors closing at the front of the house followed by a knock on the door a moment later.

'Who's that?' I ask, not expecting any visitors. As Guy goes to answer it I grab the remote and turn the TV off before the news can come back on. I'm glad that I did because the living room door opens and two police officers walk in. It's Finch and Fox again, the pair who spoke to us just after Tracey Burton had threatened me.

But what the hell are they doing back here now?

I'm fearing the worst as I stare at their uniforms and wonder if they will soon be pulling out a pair of handcuffs to put on my wrists, and as Guy follows them into the room, I see that he is afraid too because he has gone very pale.

'Sorry to disturb you this evening,' PC Finch says as he smiles at Jacob before looking at me.

'What's going on?' I ask, wondering if this is the part where Jacob has to watch both his parents being dragged away to spend the rest of their lives in custody.

'I'm sure you have heard the news by now, but if not, then the body of Mason Burton was discovered today on the old Kerrigan Industrial Estate.'

Finch pauses a moment to gauge all of our reactions, but I think I do a passable job of acting appropriately, doing my best to look sad and still surprised but also aware of current events.

'Er, yeah, we've been watching the news,' Guy admits, and Finch nods while PC Fox wanders over to the window and takes up a position there as if blocking a possible escape route, not that I'm hoping any of us is going to have a reason to need to make a run for it.

'Yes, terrible thing, it really is,' Finch says. 'Do you mind if I take a seat?'

He gestures to the space on the sofa beside me, and while I'm extremely uncomfortable at the prospect of having a police officer so close, considering what I know about what happened to Mason, him sitting down has to be better than him arresting me, so I nod my head.

Once seated, PC Finch takes a deep breath and explains why he is here.

'Right now, we are treating Mason's death as murder,' he says solemnly. 'And while there is no suspect in the case yet, we are talking to anybody who had any dealings with Mason in the days preceding his death.'

'Why?' Guy asks, slowly lowering himself into the seat beside Jacob.

'We are trying to build up a picture of his recent movements. The people he interacted with. Things he might have said. Anything that could help us figure out how he ended up losing his life.'

'How did he die?' Jacob asks, displaying that morbid fascination that so many youngsters are known for.

'We're not going to divulge that information at this time,' Finch replies. 'But we would like to ask you a few questions if that's all right?'

'You want to question Jacob?' I ask, feeling very defensive about my son and almost wishing they were questioning me instead.

'Yes, I believe you were involved in an incident with the deceased last weekend. Is that right?' Finch says, keeping his eyes on my son.

'Er, yeah, that's right,' he replies, the markings all over his face surely enough evidence of that incident as it is. 'He attacked me in the park while I was with friends.'

'I'm sorry about that,' Finch says coolly. 'Did you see Mason Burton after that?'

'No, I didn't.'

'He was in hospital after the attack,' Guy chips in then. 'We all were. As you can see, our son was in a bad way, and he's only just recently got home.'

'I appreciate that,' Finch says before taking out that damn notepad of his again. 'And I'm very grateful to you for letting us talk to you at this time. I just have a couple more questions, if that's all right?'

Jacob nods his head, making me feel proud of him and how brave he is being, because it can't be easy to be asked things by a police officer while he's still recovering from a traumatic event.

'Did Mason say anything to you during the attack? Or hint at anything happening this week?'

'No,' Jacob says. 'Nothing.'

'And how did he seem to you when you saw him?'

'You mean when he was punching me in the face?'

'Well, not quite, but I suppose so. Was he angry, upset, scared?'

'He was angry.'

'What are you getting at here, officer?' Guy asks. 'What have these questions got to do with Mason's body being found?'

'Like I said, we're just trying to build up a picture of Mason's mental state in the last few days of his life. Trying to map out as many of his movements as we can.'

'Why?' Jacob asks.

'Because if we can get a full picture, then we might be able to figure out who did this to him,' Fox says, suddenly speaking. 'Somebody around here knows something, and as you and your family had plenty of dealings with Mason Burton in the days leading up to his death, we will have a number of questions to ask you. Not all today, but we will most likely be back again.'

That last sentence sends a shiver down my spine, and I see Guy noticeably flinch as well but, thankfully, neither officer seems to notice it. When they go to leave, I'm grateful that I haven't even seen so much as a glimpse of a pair of handcuffs since they've been here. But, like PC Fox said, they will be back with more questions, and once the police have gone and Jacob has left the living room to go to the toilet, Guy explains why they are interested in us.

'They'll be talking to anybody who they think might have had a motive to hurt Mason,' he says, keeping his voice low so Jacob doesn't overhear. 'And from their point of view, all three of us did.'

'Oh god,' I say, feeling like I'm going to be sick. 'We're suspects?'

'Not yet,' Guy replies, going over to the window and peering out to make sure that the police are definitely leaving. 'But I'm sure we'll be on the list at some point when they draw up the names of anybody who Mason might have made an enemy out of.'

'So what does that mean?'

'I don't know,' Guy replies, still looking out at the front of the house even though the police have driven off. But then he lets me know why. He's looking at the driveway, or rather, what is parked on the driveway.

'I need to get rid of our car,' he says quietly but decisively. 'And I need to do it before the police come back.'

As I stare at the car too, I know my husband is right. Any and all evidence has to be taken care of now that the police are sniffing around us. That's the only way we can not only keep our secret safe, but keep our family together at the same time.

But can we do it?

It'd be tough for a master criminal, but two people who barely know what they are doing?

We're going to need all the luck we can get.

Even then, that might not be enough.

THIRTY

GUY

I'm leaving the house to go and get some much-needed exercise after neglecting all aspects of my health in these recent stressful times and, as I lock the front door and head up the driveway, I pass my new car, the one I've only had for a couple of days. Most importantly, the one that was not involved in the abduction of Mason Burton.

Having been spooked by the police officers coming to our house and talking to Jacob the other day, I decided that it was not worth the risk of keeping my old car any longer, because if the police were to put any of us on some kind of suspects list, then the next time they called by, they might be accompanied by a number of forensic experts. If so, all it would take was for them to go hunting for Mason's DNA in the back of that car and, once they found it, they would surely like to know why it was there. There is no obvious answer to that question, and from there, it would be pretty easy to see how I would end up in custody as the prime suspect in the murder of the person who beat up my son.

So the car has gone, traded in, a deal done with a slightly dodgy automobile website in which it's more about cash exchanging hands than it is about making sure all the correct paperwork is in place. I got a terrible deal in the sale, losing money overall, but the main thing is that the car was not only taken with no questions asked but will be moved on quickly and in a deal that won't leave much of a paper trail.

My new motor is not as fun to drive or as fun to look at, but it's evidence-free, and should the police ever ask me why I changed my car, I will tell them that my wife and I now work from home nearly all the time, so we didn't need to be spending so much money on our old vehicle. There's no reason why they wouldn't believe that and, even if they didn't, the car is long gone now anyway.

Feeling much better about that side of things, I make my way on foot towards the local park, keen to stretch my legs and just as keen to have a break from Sara and her constant worrying about what might happen next. I know I have been paranoid about things, as evidenced by my changing vehicles, but at least when I am paranoid I actually do something productive about it. Sara, on the other hand, just worries herself into a frenzy for no other reason than because she can, and she unloads all that stress and anxiety on to me. But I've got enough on my plate to deal with and am barely keeping it together myself, so I'm getting away for an hour or so, and when I return to the house, I hope to be feeling a little bit more optimistic about things. And despite everything that's happened, there are certainly reasons to have some optimism.

Though it didn't go down exactly how we thought it would, Mason Burton is no longer around to trouble Jacob or any other person, and good riddance to him. As well as that, whoever killed him saved Sara and me the hassle of having to persuade Mason to keep quiet about us threatening him. It would have been hard, if not impossible, to trust Mason if we'd let him go, but it was obvious that neither Sara nor I could have killed him if need be, so we didn't have much choice there.

That killer, whoever they may be and wherever they may be hiding now, did everyone a favour.

I wonder what their reasons were for killing Mason. They must have been pretty strong to take such decisive and violent action. I guess they had been tracking Mason's movements too, just like I did. The thought that whoever they are saw me while they were keeping an eye on Mason is troubling. But best not to dwell on all that too much on such a fine day as this. As I enter the park, I smile at the sight of several other residents of this town enjoying the outdoor leisure space.

There are numerous dogs running around chasing tennis balls thrown by their owners, a few kids kicking a football around and using their sweatshirts for goalposts, and there are even a few couples who have decided that it's the perfect weather for a picnic, sitting on the grass on a blanket full of food items, nibbling away and whispering sweet nothings in one another's ears.

Everybody here looks like they don't have a care in the world, and it's nice to be around them and remind myself that it's not all doom and gloom. But as I make my way around the path that circles this popular park, I catch a glimpse of the bushes behind which Jacob was attacked by Mason when that little terror was still alive. It's my first time coming down here since that incident and, even though it's in the past, it does taint my experience of being here somewhat. I wonder if and when Jacob will ever be able to come back down here himself and enjoy this park again, after what he went through the last time he was here. That remains to be seen, but one thing is for sure.

Mason Burton will never get to enjoy this park again.

I pass the scene of my son's attack and try not to dwell on it any longer, choosing instead to watch two female friends throwing a frisbee to one another a hundred yards away from me or so. But it's because I'm paying attention to them that I fail to see who is approaching me on this path until they are standing right in front of me.

'Guy? Hey, it's good to see you.'

I see Kevin Atkinson smiling at me, the first time I've seen this man since we shared a drink in the pub after football, and he confessed to having plenty of regret over how things happened regarding Mason and his late daughter.

'Oh, hi, Kevin. How are you doing?'

I shake his hand then, more to be polite than because I feel like we're actually old friends, but once we do, I notice that Kevin really is looking happy. Far happier than the last time we were together anyway.

'I'm great, thanks for asking. How are you?'

'Er, yeah, I'm all right. Just enjoying this nice weather.'

'Lovely, isn't it? If only the sun came out more often.'

'Yeah, that would be good.'

I'm wondering if we are going to have much to talk about besides the weather, but at least it's a cheerier topic than the last time we conversed. But then Kevin takes a step closer to me and speaks in more hushed tones.

'Is it me, or does the world feel a better place today than it did a few days ago?'

It only takes me a second to realise what he is referring to, but I say nothing, wondering if he is going to elaborate on his point. And, sure enough, he does.

'It's as if the air is cleaner, like there's less pollution around or something. Do you get what I mean?'

I think I do, but I still say nothing.

'I don't know about you, but I feel much better about things these days,' Kevin goes on. 'I guess you could say I've turned the corner, and the worst is behind me. I'm very grateful for that, just as I'm grateful for meeting you.'

With that, Kevin extends his hand again, and even though

we've already shaken once today, he obviously wants to do so again.

I take his hand and shake, but as I do, he leans in even closer to me and tells me that his daughter can rest in peace now that thug is no longer around. Then he winks at me before letting go of my hand, bidding me farewell and walking away.

I watch him go, noting the spring in his step and the cheerfulness in his demeanour, as well as remembering the sly wink he just gave me as we shook hands.

There's no doubt about it, Kevin is a happier man than the last time I saw him, and it seems it's all because of Mason's death. But was he just slyly hinting at something there? Is there something else he is happy about?

Something like getting away with murder, perhaps?

As I stand and watch Kevin leaving the park, I can't help but ask myself one question.

Was it Kevin who snuck into that warehouse and killed Mason before Sara and I had finished with him?

THIRTY-ONE

SARA

I'm aware that my husband has gone for a walk around the park, not for exercise but because he wants a break from me, but I don't mind that because I could do with a break from him myself, if I'm honest. The pair of us being cooped up in this house and worrying about what the police might be looking into is not a good combination, so a bit of breathing space is probably the best thing for us both. But I've been thinking about something else that might help not just us but the rest of our family too, and that's why I'm now sitting in front of my laptop and browsing several travel company websites.

We all need a holiday.

It's four weeks until Jacob will be on his school break again, and once he is I want to cheer him up by taking him somewhere he can escape from it all. He's been through some awful things recently, and a bit of family time in the sun will be just the medicine. He can kick his football around on a beach, swim in the sea or the pool and, most of all, forget about things like school, teenage stresses and his horrible history with Mason Burton. But Guy and I could do with a change of scene as well, if only because putting a bit of distance between us and this town for a couple of weeks will hopefully push the memories of the last time we saw Mason a little further back into our brains. I'll be sure to invite Amber too, although her coming with us might depend on how much fun she is having at university, her course workload and whether or not she can fit a little bit of sunbathing into her hectic lifestyle. It'll be great if she can come so all four of us are there, but I won't hold my breath. As long as the three of us can get away, that will be fine by me.

I'm still very much at that early stage of pre-booking a holiday, where I spend less time thinking about the budget and more time admiring dozens of dazzling photos of hotels, pools and beaches, when I hear the front door open. Guy is back and, when he enters the kitchen, I expect him to ask me what I'm doing on the laptop. But he doesn't. He just stares at me blankly to the point where he starts to give me the creeps.

'What is it? What's happened now?' I ask him, all images of sun-soaked beaches disappearing from my brain as all my worries and anxieties about the police come flooding back.

'I saw Kevin Atkinson in the park,' he says. 'He came up to me and greeted me like we were best friends.'

'And?'

'Well, it was a bit strange.'

'What did he say?'

'Weird stuff.'

'Like what?'

Guy pulls out one of the chairs and sits down at the table. Sensing that what I am about to hear might be troubling, I close the laptop and put the holiday planning on the back burner.

'He was talking about the world being a better place now,' Guy says. 'Cleaner air. Less pollution.'

'What?'

'Then he said he felt better about things.'

'Things?'

'Like what happened with Zoe. He said he had turned the corner, was moving on.'

'That's good.'

'Maybe.'

Guy still looks very troubled, so I reach out and put my hand on top of his to urge him to just go ahead and get whatever it is off his chest.

'Then he leaned in and told me Zoe could rest in peace now that Mason was no longer around.'

I think about that, and while it might make sense on the face of it, it's obvious there could be much more to it than that.

'Then he winked at me,' Guys adds. 'He winked as if he had some kind of secret and was letting me in on it. And what if he was?'

'A secret?'

'What if he is the one who killed Mason?'

'You think he did?'

'I don't know for sure, but he seemed to be dropping some pretty big hints. All that stuff about the world being a better place now, his daughter being able to rest in peace. I think he might have killed him!'

'Woah, calm down. Do you think Kevin is capable of murder?'

'I wouldn't have thought so before that conversation, but yeah, now I'm pretty convinced.'

'But why would he tell you?'

'Well, he didn't come and confess to it as such, but he was hinting, and I suppose if it was him, he knows that we're the ones who threatened Mason and we were two of the last people to see him alive. So it might have been his way of thanking me for helping him get rid of that bully.'

'But how could he do that? I mean, how would he have known we were going to abduct Mason and go to the warehouse? He'd have to have been following us, right?'

'I guess so.'

'But why would he do that?'

'Maybe he thought I was going to do something after our little chat. He knew what Mason was doing to Jacob, and maybe he could tell that I was thinking about taking action.'

I think about all this, and while what Guy is saying might be somewhat plausible, it's still a bit of a reach to think it could actually be true.

'But wait,' I say, racking my brain for all possible explanations or ways to dismiss this idea. 'Mason hurt Zoe three years ago. If Kevin wanted to kill him, why wait until now?'

'He told me he wished he had done something sooner. Maybe talking to me stirred up those feelings again or something. I don't know. All I do know is that Kevin is happy that Mason is dead, and he wanted me to know it!'

'Okay, so now you know it,' I say. 'But let's think about this for a moment. Say Kevin is the one who killed Mason. Would that be such a bad thing?'

Now it's Guy's turn to ask me the questions.

'What do you mean?'

'Well, if Kevin is the killer, he's your friend, and he's on our side. He knows exactly what we have been through with Mason's bullying of our son. You guys had a heart-to-heart in the pub. He likes you. Therefore, even if he knows we're the ones who threatened Mason before he died, he isn't likely to share that information with anybody, is he?'

Guy turns this over in his mind before coming around to my way of thinking.

'I guess not,' he says.

'And if you think about it, it makes sense,' I go on, warming to my theme. 'If there was one person in this town who wanted Mason dead more than us the other day, then it was Kevin, right? Three years of agony; three years of mourning his daughter. Eventually, it all got too much for him, and when he saw we

were going to act, he decided it was his last chance to do something himself, so he swooped in and killed Mason. It all makes
sense, doesn't it?'

'I suppose.'

'Then everything's going to be okay,' I go on, feeling more
confident by the second. 'Kevin got justice for his daughter.
He's not going to report us. And we're not going to go to prison.'

I am waiting for Guy to agree with me and, once he does,
I'll be able to improve his mood even further by telling him all
about my holiday plans. But he holds off for a moment and looks
quite pensive, though I'm not quite sure why.

'Let's not get too excited just yet,' he says to me, and I notice
that he's looking over my shoulder, so I turn around and see
what he is seeing through the window.

Once again, we have more unwanted guests at our house.

The police are back.

But there are a lot more of them than last time.

THIRTY-TWO

GUY

Having a team of police officers and forensic experts swarming all over my property would have been extremely daunting if I was innocent. But being in this position while I was harbouring guilt made it ten times worse.

It's been a week since the horrible day when every part of my family's home was unexpectedly examined, every cupboard drawer and door opened and every room infiltrated by those in uniform, but, even with the passage of that amount of time, the stress of it has not worn off yet.

I was convinced that Sara and I were screwed when I opened the door and was immediately shown a warrant that gave the officers permission to make a search of our house and, despite asking them why they were here and felt they had to do such a thing, it took a little while before I got some answers.

The police had been stepping up their investigation into who had killed Mason, and having drawn up a list of anybody in town who they felt had a motive, they were taking decisive action and paying all those suspects a visit. Sara and I fell into that category, all thanks to Dean and Tracey Burton mentioning our names when the police had asked them if they could think of anybody who might have wished to harm their son. That meant the police had free rein to turn our things upside down in a bid to find any shred of evidence that might prove we were at that warehouse and had something to do with Mason's untimely demise.

I had kept my arm around my wife to try and keep her calm as the police had run roughshod over the home we had so lovingly formed together, and I had also been called upon to try and quell Jacob's fears when his bedroom was so dramatically entered too. The three of us had huddled in the hallway and watched the investigation unfolding before our very eyes, although only two of us had been aware that the police were actually much closer to finding out the truth than they realised.

Jacob was the only one who was genuinely angry about what was happening. I had to feign my anger, as did Sara, acting shocked and disgusted at the happenings but secretly knowing that the police partly were on the right track, although not fully. Yes, we were kidnappers, but we hadn't killed Mason, and it was during the raid on our home that I considered telling the police about my conversation with Kevin Atkinson in the park.

The idea of getting the police to stop looking here and instead go looking at him was a tempting one, but it also came laced with the risk that if he was involved in Mason's death, and ended up panicking during the search of his house, he might just tell them that he saw me and Sara at the warehouse too, and then we'd be screwed anyway. So, in the end, I kept quiet until the police had finished.

But I sure was glad I got rid of my old car and had a new one because, as I had feared, the police did make a sweep of my vehicle for any evidence of Mason's DNA. But, of course, they did not find any because that DNA was hundreds of miles away in my old car by then.

The police had eventually left us alone that day, and I took the fact that I wasn't in handcuffs as a good sign that they hadn't found anything to concern them. I've also taken the fact that a full week has gone by since then without seeing any police officers at my door as another good sign that maybe, just maybe, we are no longer on their suspect list. But I guess they will always be looking as long as Mason's murder is unsolved, and at present that is still the case.

But I can't spend all my time worrying about what may or may not happen. As I've repeatedly told my wife, we have to carry on as normal and not arouse suspicion, and that is why I am attending my regular game of Thursday night football again. However, it doesn't quite provide the respite I needed from all my worries when, no sooner have I stepped on the pitch, than one of my mates brings up a name I have become all too familiar with recently.

'Did you guys hear about Kevin Atkinson?' Chuckles asks us as he pulls on a red bib before the game. 'The police arrested him today. Turned up at his house and marched him right out of there in handcuffs. Our Kath heard it from one of his neighbours.'

My heart skips a beat as I process what my friend has just said.

'Kevin's been arrested?'

'Yeah, I guess they think he was the one who killed Mason Burton,' Chuckles replies, having a little more difficulty with his bib than a man his age should.

'Here, let me help you with that,' Baz says, offering some assistance, but he's only joking, and instead of helping Chuckles get the bib over his head, he ends up making it more difficult for him, completely on purpose, of course.

Everyone laughs; everyone except me because I'm thinking about Kevin being in custody now. All the questions he will be facing, all the possible answers he might be giving and, more specifically, whether or not he saw Sara and me that day too.

'So what's happened? Did he actually do it?' I ask nervously as the bib finally gets sorted. 'Did he kill Mason?'

'I don't know, but, apparently, he hasn't come home yet, so I guess the police are still questioning him.'

'Well, if he did do it, then he is a hero in my eyes,' Fruit Loop says as he inspects tonight's match ball. 'After what that bully did to his daughter, he had it coming to him.'

'Yeah, if anyone bullied my daughter into killing herself, then I'd have to take matters into my own hands too,' Simmo chips in, and it seems all my mates are in agreement about that.

'The problem is, even if he is a hero of a father who acted to avenge his little girl, the police won't see it like that,' Chuckles adds. 'I mean, I get why he might have done it, but still, he'll spend the rest of his life behind bars now he's been caught.'

I feel sick. I need to get out of here.

I need to go home and tell Sara what has happened.

Realising that I need an excuse to get out of this game so I can get out of here, I think about feigning an injury, but my mates might not accept that and just tell me to try and run it off. I need another excuse, an excuse that nobody will want to question me about.

'I'm really sorry, guys, but I'm going to have to go,' I say, suddenly clutching my stomach and pulling a strained face.

'What's wrong?' Baz asks me as our opponents begin filtering onto the pitch nearby.

'I think there was something wrong with the lasagne Sara made for dinner just before I came out,' I say, making sure to wince as well as crossing my legs slightly. 'I think I've got a bit of food poisoning coming on.'

If there's one thing that people don't require further elaboration on, it's the fact that somebody they know might be about to have explosive diarrhoea, so my mates just wish me well as I run from the pitch, get in my car and speed away.

. . .

But, of course, there is no food poisoning, although I still act as if I need to get into my house as quickly as possible by the way I park on the driveway and race through my front door.

'Sara!' I call out as I enter, and I find her in the living room watching some soap opera on TV. Thankfully, Jacob is not sitting with her, so I can talk freely.

'What's wrong? Why aren't you at football?' she asks me, hitting the pause button on the remote control.

'The police have arrested Kevin!' I cry as I struggle to catch my breath. Ironically, I wouldn't be this out of breath if I had stayed and played that game of football.

'What?'

'I heard it from Chuckles. Apparently, one of Kevin's neighbours saw him being taken into custody in handcuffs. They think he's the one who killed Mason.'

'But what evidence do they have?'

'I don't know. Maybe they searched his house like they searched ours. They obviously figured out he had a motive.'

'Oh my god, he must have done it then.'

'But what if he mentions us?'

'He won't, will he? He's your friend.'

'He probably didn't think he would get caught. Who knows what he'll say now to try and get out of it.'

'What's going on?' Jacob asks, and I spin around to see him standing in the doorway behind me.

Did he hear us?

'Nothing,' I say, trying to play it cool. 'What's going on with you?'

'I've just read that Kevin Atkinson has been charged with Mason's murder,' Jacob says. 'It's all over the news.'

He grabs the remote control from his mother then and changes the channel until he finds one showing the news. And there it is. Confirmation on the screen that Kevin Atkinson has not just been arrested. He has been charged. The police must believe they have their man.

'Did he admit to it?' I ask, thinking about how it was only a short time ago that Kevin was walking around in the park as a free man. But not any more.

'I read online that the police found evidence at his house,' Jacob tells me. 'Someone posted it in a True Crime Facebook group, and then one of my friends sent it to me. He must have done it. He killed Mason.'

The three of us watch the footage on the screen, though it's not showing much. Just a few images of the warehouse followed by some footage of Kevin's home, though the man himself is not in any of the images. That's because he's in a police cell now, facing all these charges.

But there is one clip of him that eventually gets shown. It's an historic one from just after his daughter had died three years ago, and a journalist had thrust a microphone in his face and asked him for his thoughts on Mason's bullying. What he says has quite cleverly been selected for inclusion in this bulletin here by the news channel editor because it's very telling.

Kevin simply said four words back then.

'This is not over.'

I guess it's taken three years for him to prove himself right.

THIRTY-THREE

SARA

This nightmare goes on. Kevin is maintaining his innocence and refusing to plead guilty.

So now there has to be a trial.

Unsurprisingly, the trial promises to be the biggest news story this town has ever seen and, because of that, journalists and other members of the media have descended on these usually quiet streets, turning this part of the map into the epicentre of the country, until a verdict is reached by a jury anyway. But before that can happen, the prosecution and the defence will have their say, and as lawyers, police officers, family members and members of the general public make their way up the steps into the courthouse, I am amongst them because I want to hear everything that is said in this trial.

Guy advised against it, telling me I shouldn't show my face here, but I told him that if I didn't, then we might never know the full story of what really went on in that warehouse. We only know half the story, which is that we took Mason and put him in harm's way. But we still don't know exactly how he ended up coming to harm, and if Kevin insists that he is innocent, maybe he is and, if so, that would mean the killer is still out there somewhere.

But I am aware that it might have seemed suspicious to be here following the trial, so I made sure to rekindle my friendship with Kevin's wife, Mary, over these last few months while her husband has been in custody awaiting his day in court. I told her that I had great sympathy for what she was going through, as well as a history of my own with Mason Burton, and it was clear she needed a shoulder to cry on with everything that was going on, so I made sure to provide that shoulder. As we grew closer, I told her I would do anything she needed me to do to help her get through this ordeal, and when she asked me to be present during the trial as a friendly face in the courtroom, I gratefully accepted. That secured me my spot in the court, and based on how long the queue was for the public gallery this morning, it was most likely the only way I would have got a space in here, because this is an event that is turning out to be the hottest ticket in town.

The benches in this courtroom are packed as everybody gets into place at the behest of the judge, and I can only imagine that will add to the nerves that are already jangling around in Kevin's body when he is led in here in handcuffs any moment now.

I see Mary sitting down near the front alongside her daughter, Erica, and she's already dabbing at her eyes with a tissue, which doesn't bode well because proceedings haven't even got underway yet. But she really starts crying when we all get our first glimpse of the accused as he is marched into the dock with two police officers flanking his every beleaguered move.

Kevin looks drawn and haggard, and his movements are slow and stiff. From here, he does not look very much like a man capable of murder. But perhaps he is just making himself look like this to garner sympathy from the twelve members of the jury, or maybe he is just in shock, having presumed he might never get caught for what he did on that fateful day. But he's in the dock now, and once the judge gets things underway, he faces a battle to prove his innocence, if that is indeed what he intends to do. And he does, stating his 'not guilty' plea quietly but loudly enough for everybody in the room to hear it. With that, the trial commences.

Like everybody else in the courtroom, I am wondering if Kevin really is guilty or not, but unlike everybody else here, I know I played a part in the events that occurred on the day that Mason Burton died. That is why it is extremely difficult for me to listen as the prosecution go over the details of the case, outlining everything from how Mason died, the site where his body was found before moving on to why Kevin Atkinson is the prime suspect in this case, crucial evidence that puts the accused at the scene of the crime. In this instance, that evidence consisted of the discovery of an incriminating item, but it's only when it's read out in court that I learn what it is for the very first time.

When I do, it takes all my composure not to let out a gasp.

It was the rope Guy and I tied up Mason with.

Apparently, the police discovered it bundled up at the back of Kevin's garage, and when the forensics had examined it in the lab, they discovered the red stain on one of the ropes was a drop of Mason's blood. As far as the police were concerned, then, they had their man. But I know that Guy took that rope home and put it in the bin in our house, and the following day the rubbish was collected, removing it for good.

Or so I thought.

But it seems not unless Kevin really did do it and somehow took some of the rope without us noticing before we went back inside the warehouse. But that seems unlikely, doesn't it? Either way, that is the crucial piece of evidence on which it seems this entire case hangs, and once all the details surrounding it have been explained to the court, the cross-examination of the accused begins.

Predictably, the prosecution's first question is to ask how the rope with Mason's blood on it came to be on Kevin's property and, just as predictably, Kevin does not have a good answer for that one. He just denies knowing about its existence and says however it got there, it wasn't put there by him. Then he makes a rather valid point. Even if he had killed Mason, why would he store a piece of evidence linking himself to the crime in his garage for the police to come along and potentially find one day? But, of course, Kevin wouldn't be the first criminal to try and explain away something incriminating by making it seem like he wouldn't be so stupid and that there must be another explanation.

But the fact that Kevin has always had a strong motive to want to hurt Mason is a motive that the prosecution quickly touch on by asking the accused all about his late daughter and the circumstances surrounding her death.

It's painful to have to listen to Kevin recount the details of Zoe's bullying, suicide and the impact all that had on his life, and even though his lawyer would have surely advised against it, Kevin does admit that there were plenty of times when he wished Mason would come to harm. A few people in the public gallery wince when he says that, as do one or two members of the jury, but Kevin then insists that it was only ever wishing, and he never actually laid a finger on Mason. But the prosecution are all over that admission, almost as much as they focus on the rope in the garage, and in this case it seems Kevin has been too honest. But that makes me think even more he might not be guilty, because if he is clearly too honest for his own good, he wouldn't stand up in court and lie about being innocent.

However, the incriminating rope is a huge problem, and that's even more obvious when the defence gets to have their say in the following days of the trial, because despite whatever arguments they might come up with, it is a tough sell to try and persuade the jury that Mason's blood on Kevin's property is not a big problem. But they do raise a key point of defence that might help the accused, and that is the fact he apparently has a cast-iron alibi for around the time period that Mason would have been killed. He and Mary were away in Cardiff for a couple of nights, visiting Erica, their remaining daughter, where she studies at university, and there is plenty of CCTV evidence of him and his car in the city during the period Mason is believed to have been taken to the warehouse and killed. While the prosecution had suggested Kevin could have driven back at any point during that trip to Cardiff to commit the crime before returning to the Welsh capital, extensive studying of the road traffic cameras in various places along the routes he might have taken do not show his vehicle. Instead, they show it only in Cardiff, and he is at the wheel with his wife beside him. The alibi seems strong, which obviously gives Kevin and his family hope in this case, as well as gives me room to worry that this case may be about to be left open. That worry only intensifies when a member of the defence suggests a theory, one that could be plausible and explain why the incriminating ropes ended up at Kevin's house. They suggest that the rope could have been planted in Kevin's garage by another person, the real killer, and a person who wanted to lay the blame at Kevin's door, knowing full well that he would always be one of the first suspects in this case anyway.

That is something to consider and consider it I do as the trial rumbles on. The idea of the rope being planted sticks with me for the rest of the trial, not only when I'm watching on in court but when I'm at home with my family or lying in bed and enduring yet another sleepless night. But the most troubling part of it all is that I know that rope was originally put in our bin at the back of the house, and it was put there by Guy. Therefore, we were the only two people who knew about its existence and its location. I know for certain that I did not move that rope and put it on Kevin's property, which means it only leaves one other person who could have done it.

Did Guy move that rope before the rubbish was collected?

Did he plant the evidence at Kevin's in a bid to frame him?

And, if so, what the hell was he thinking?

I know I should ask him, just come right out with it and demand to know the truth. But I'm terrified of what the answer might be. That's why I stay quiet during all those long nights at home, and I stay even quieter during the long days in court as the trial reaches its conclusion, and by the time it's done and both the prosecution and the defence have made their closing statements, I know it is far too late to raise any concerns I might have. That's because the jury retires to consider their verdicts and, having heard both sides of the argument, it is they and only they who can decide Kevin's fate now.

And decide it they do.

That's because the jury quickly reach a unanimous verdict when they are asked for one.

And that is the moment Kevin Atkinson is found not guilty of the murder of Mason Burton.

THIRTY-FOUR

GUY

I had already heard about the verdict before Sara got home to tell me about it. That's because it was plastered all over the news broadcasts and for good reason, because it's not every day that this town has a story to report on like this one. But I've been trying to avoid watching too many of the news reports because I have no wish to exhibit a morbid fascination with this whole sorry tale.

I also have no wish in further worrying about who might have really killed Mason now that Kevin has just been found not guilty of that crime.

I guess Kevin did not kill Mason, which was partly a relief when I found out, because I do not wish prison time on that poor man after what he has already been through. But it's a cause for concern, too, because it means the real killer is still at large.

Or are they? Having met Kevin myself and seen how hard he took the loss of his daughter, I always felt immense sympathy for him. But so could a jury. What if they have simply afforded Kevin the benefit of the doubt in this case, and, after considering all he has been through with the loss of his daughter, they went a little easier on him and opted to find him not guilty, even if they had a few doubts of their own? I'm sure it wouldn't be the first time a jury had found themselves thinking they might have done something bad if they were in the shoes of the accused. But, then again, maybe they genuinely believe what appears to be the newest theory in this case, and that is a theory I hear all about when Sara comes home after the verdict and immediately asks me if I had anything to do with the ropes being found on Kevin's property.

'What? You've got to be kidding?' I say, exasperated at my wife's nonsensical suggestion. 'You think I framed Kevin?'

'You put those ropes in our rubbish bin, yet somehow they ended up in his garage,' Sara cries, able to speak as loudly and as freely as she wants because Jacob is back at school now, and we have the house to ourselves. 'I didn't take them out of the bin, and you were the only other person who knew about their existence!'

'But why on earth would I want to set up Kevin? Listen to yourself, it makes absolutely no sense.'

'Doesn't it? What if you were worried we might get caught for what we did, so you tried to deflect the attention elsewhere? You might have panicked. Did you panic?'

'No, I did not! I put the ropes in the bin, and the rubbish was collected the following day. That was the end of it as far as I was concerned, and it's downright insulting that you won't believe me!'

I'm furious at Sara for even thinking I could be capable of such a thing as potentially framing an innocent man. Not only that, she isn't taking my word for what I'm saying, which is not the behaviour a loyal, loving wife should be displaying.

'I can't believe you don't trust me,' I say, hurt deeply by all of this, though I also know that Sara has a point. Those ropes somehow got from this house to Kevin's, and that is unexplained.

'Well, if you didn't try to frame him, then somebody else must have done it,' Sara decides. 'Unless Kevin was the killer, saw us at the warehouse and watched you hide the ropes and thought to himself, no, I'll take them back to my place instead and give the police a real easy job. But not only is that incredibly unrealistic, it's also impossible because he was in Cardiff at that time!'

Now Sara is getting sarcastic, and that's not going to help anybody.

'He must have done it,' I say, scratching my head, even though it seems he was many miles away in Wales while Sara and I were the ones dragging Mason off the street and tying him up. 'There has to be a way he did it.'

'I don't know, Guy. All I know is that I saw Kevin in that courtroom, and he did not look like a guilty man.'

'But what if he is? I mean, he's had three years to get himself to a point where he might have perfected an "innocent guy" act. Maybe appearances are deceptive. Maybe I completely misjudged him when I first met him, and he wasn't as powerless and timid as I thought. Maybe he's smarter than everybody. Us, the police, the jury. Everyone.'

The truth is that I would have thought Kevin being found guilty would have finally brought an end to all of this, but now that hasn't happened, I can see that is not the case, especially so because Sara seems so determined to get to the bottom of what really happened. But I have a warning for her.

'You need to drop this,' I tell her. 'You can't go around spouting off theories or asking any more questions. If you do, the police will start looking at us again, and we can't risk that. We seem to have got away with what we did, and we have to try and keep it that way.'

'But something's not right.'

'There's a lot about this that isn't right, Sara, including you not trusting me. But the last time I checked, we committed a crime, and we got away with it. So just drop it!'

I leave the room then, hoping I've made my message loud and clear and there is no further need for discussion. And in the following days and weeks, it seems I have because Sara never mentions her qualms about Kevin's case ever again. She doesn't even say anything when a news bulletin one night mentions that the family home of Kevin Atkinson was vandalised, an act that ends up being attributed to a member of the Burton family.

Apparently, one of Mason's cousins decided to get busy with a can of spray paint, graffitiing all sorts of nasty words on the walls of Kevin's home. But it was a reminder of several things, including the fact that this town would not forget what had happened easily and also that Mason's family were far from angels themselves. However, it was also a reminder of how much the people in this town sympathise with the plight of Kevin and his family, because no sooner had the graffiti been reported on than dozens of volunteers from the town arrived at the scene, armed with buckets of water and brushes, and they spent the next several hours cleaning the graffiti off.

It was perhaps this new reminder of how much trouble the Burton family were that resulted in my punishment for the charges of trespassing, harassment and assault against Dean Burton being dropped down to a fine and community service. It was a huge relief when I found out I would not have to serve a custodial sentence for punching that man, and it was a further relief when my employer told me that they were willing to have me back in the office, providing I had no more brushes with the law. The good news only kept on coming when we heard that Dean and Tracey Burton had decided to move out of town, apparently looking to get over the loss of their son elsewhere, and I knew that them leaving would only pour more water onto the raging fire that had been burning in this place ever since their son had first started bullying poor Zoe.

As time went by and the dust began to settle on everything that had happened, it seemed like my family and I had managed to come out of it all relatively unscathed, barring a few psychological scars, of course. The main thing, as far as Sara and I were concerned, was that Jacob was enjoying his school life again, and he could go and play in the park with his friends without fear of being attacked and ending up in hospital again. It was our desire to protect him that started this whole thing, but with his health and safety assured now, I could rest much easier in my role as a parent and, all in all, we had to consider ourselves fortunate that things worked out well for our family.

But while the passage of time was making things easier, there was one more thing that promised to help and that was the upcoming holiday that Sara had booked for the four of us. We were headed to Cyprus just as soon as Jacob's and Amber's respective term times had concluded, and all four of us could not wait for some good weather and a change of scene. I also hoped that it would be the thing that would finally start to bring Sara and me closer together again. The cracks in our relationship that had formed over recent months were still there, but hopefully still very much repairable, with just a little bit of effort on both of our parts.

And so, as the day of the holiday rolled around, and I helped the taxi driver put our suitcases into the back of the cab before we all departed for the airport, I was full of optimism and excitement for the future. If we'd survived everything that could happen here in this town in recent times, surely we could get through a ten-day break in Cyprus without any dramas. I know Sara was thinking the same thing too.

But were we right?

AFTER

THIRTY-FIVE

SARA

It's a balmy thirty-three degrees, and it's not even midday yet, not that I'm complaining as I reach for the bottle of sunscreen that my husband has just finished applying to himself. Bless him, Guy has made a good attempt at protecting himself from the sun's rays by applying a healthy dose of lotion, but he is sweating so much that I fear much of it is just coming straight off before it's even had a chance to soak into his skin.

'I'm boiling,' he admits as he lies back on his sun lounger with his sunglasses on and a baseball cap covering his head, the visor of which is providing him with at least a little shade, although the rest of his body is very much in the sun's rays. The only thing he is wearing besides the cap and glasses is a tight pair of swim shorts, and, as he adjusts them slightly, I can see evidence of the tan lines that have formed in the five days we have been here already. But we mustn't complain about the heat because it won't be long until we're back in England, and the last time I checked, the weather there was cold and wet, as was to be expected.

'How much of this did you use?' I ask Guy as I pick up the

bottle of sunscreen and find it to be extremely light, suggesting there isn't much left in there any more.

'Do you want me to burn?' Guy replies before picking up his plastic cup full of frothy beer and taking a long, refreshing sip. I'm glad we decided to go all-inclusive with this holiday, because with the number of times my husband has been back and forth to the bar, I dread to think how much it would have cost us if he was having to pay for each one of those beers separately.

Using the last of what is left of the sunscreen, I just about manage to get my legs protected, but I know I'll need to go back to the hotel room and get another bottle if I am to protect the rest of my body from the harsh UV rays. I'll do that soon, but, for the moment, I am comfortable where I am, reclining on my own sun lounger. As I look around, I take in the various sights that are contributing to this being a fantastic holiday so far.

Right in front of me is the pool and in there are Jacob and Amber, my two children, beating the stifling heat by taking a dip in the cool water. As I watch them chatting to each other as they sit on the steps in the shallow end, I smile. It's lovely to see a brother and sister getting along so well, and with their complexions enhanced by the generous amount of Vitamin D in these parts, they both look as happy and healthy as I can remember in a long time.

Beyond them is the bar that Guy has been frequenting so much, and I can see the Cypriot bartender behind there now, pouring more drinks for some of the other guests at this four-star resort in the town of Protaras on the eastern side of this sun-kissed island. Behind that is the hotel itself, a sprawling five-storey structure painted all in white, as most buildings are around here, and I can spot a few people dotted about on the numerous balconies that overlook this pool area. Our room is up there somewhere, and I'll have to go back there shortly because I can feel myself starting to burn. Before I do, I allow my gaze to wander beyond the hotel and land on the tiny but picturesque structure on the top of the parched, brown hill in the distance.

That structure is the Profitus Ilias, a church that overlooks this town from high up on the hill and a place that my family made the walk up to on our second day here. The taxi driver who brought us from the airport to our hotel advised us to make the hike because the views at the top were worth it, and we did just that. It was a fun morning for the four of us, once we got to the top and enjoyed the vantage point, and it was made even more magical when we witnessed a young man going down on one knee and proposing to his girlfriend, who excitedly said yes. The romance of the moment was not lost on Guy or me, and we shared a knowing smile, a sign that our own strong feelings of love were starting to return after a testing time back in the UK.

Feeling like I might want to put Guy's love for me to the test right now, I lean over and ask him if he might want to go back to the room for me to get more sunscreen so I can stay where I am. But he mentions that he needs to finish his beer first before it gets too warm, so unless I want to wait for that, I'll have to go myself.

I feel like my chest is getting red, so I daren't wait any longer, and with some tutting and heavy sighing designed to make Guy feel a little bit guilty about me going back to the room instead of him, I leave the sunbeds and head inside the hotel.

My flip-flops make a soft padding sound as I cross the marble floor of the reception area before I enter one of the lifts and travel up to the fourth floor. From there, it's only a ten-second walk to Room 412. As I enter the room, I'm cooled by the air-conditioning unit blowing out cold air above my head.

I take a moment to savour the drop in temperature before I make a start on locating a new bottle of sunscreen. I'm pretty sure it's in one of the suitcases, though I can't remember which one. With there being four of us, I made sure to spread out the heavier items like sunscreen between all the cases so we stood more of a chance of not going over the baggage allowance when we checked in at the airport. But that means it could be in any one of four suitcases because none of us completely unpacked them all when we got here, so I've got a little hunting around to do.

The room we're in is a two-bedroom suite with a master bedroom that Guy and I are using, a single room that Amber has taken, and then there is a sofa bed in the main living area that Jacob crashes out on, which he doesn't mind because it means he has the TV in the same room as him, so he can stay up and watch it late at night. The layout of our accommodation means each of our suitcases is spread throughout the rooms, but after finding no more sunscreen in mine, I go to check on the children's cases. Locating no sunscreen but at least a full bottle of Aftersun in Jacob's, I make my way into Amber's room and spot her case poking out from underneath her bed.

As I pull it out, I can safely assume that what I am looking for is in here, having exhausted all other options, but before I can open her suitcase, I notice it dragging on something as I pull it out. Looking under the bed, I see that a book has become wedged, so I reach in and pick it up and it's only when I do that I realise it isn't a book but a diary.

I always knew Amber liked to do a bit of journaling in her youth, but I had no idea she had carried on with it once she'd gone to university. Despite knowing I shouldn't, I can't help but sneak a peek inside the diary. I justify it to myself by believing it will be a good way of knowing for sure if my daughter really is happy at uni, because otherwise I just have to take her word for it. If there's one thing I've learnt about children since becoming a parent, it's that they don't always tell the truth.

I open the diary at a random page and read the first couple of lines. From what I gather, Amber is describing a cute guy she has noticed in one of her lectures, and how she hopes she might see him out one night at the student nightclub, because it will be less awkward to talk to him there when they're drunk rather than in a lecture hall when they're both sober and nervous.

I smile to myself at the innocent tale before absentmindedly turning to another randomly selected page in the diary. When I read the first few lines of this next entry, it's obvious this one is nowhere near as innocent as the last.

That's because it mentions Mason Burton.

EPILOGUE
SARA

My entire body turns cold as I read the diary, but it has nothing to do with the air-con system in the hotel room and everything to do with the fact that my daughter has written some extremely disturbing things, the depths of which I only start to learn as I keep turning the pages to follow her various entries.

Just found out my little brother is being bullied by the same scumbag who bullied Zoe Atkinson into killing herself. What a low-life!

I'm driving home later from university because my brother is in hospital!! And Mason Burton put him there! I could kill him!

Went to see bro in hospital and it was horrible! His face is a mess! Mason Burton is a scumbag! And Mum and Dad look so sad. I hate what that bully has done to us and now all I can think about is how I could get revenge for my family.

It's clear that Amber hated Mason as much as the rest of us

did, but her writing words like 'revenge' and 'kill' make me feel afraid. Sure enough, my fears are founded when I read an entry that almost causes me to drop the diary as if its pages are burning my skin.

> *Could sense that something was wrong when Mum and Dad left the house really early this morning and Mum returned alone. So when she went out again in the car a little later, I followed her in mine. What I saw was crazy! Mum and Dad kidnapped Mason! I couldn't believe it, but it got worse because I followed them to some old warehouse, and by the time I'd parked up far enough away so they wouldn't see me, I crept up to the warehouse and saw they had tied Mason up with rope! WTF!*
>
> *It was then I realised that they were going to kill him because I saw Dad with a knife, but Mum stopped him just before he could stab him and said they had to talk outside. They left but the knife was still in the warehouse, and I guess adrenaline took over because the next thing I knew, I had that knife in my hand.*
>
> *I saw a way to get revenge for Jacob.*
>
> *And I did it.*
>
> *Mason Burton won't be hurting anybody else ever again and boy, did it feel good to make sure of it.*

I have to put one hand to my mouth to stop myself from being sick. But even though I manage that, it doesn't change what appear to be the facts.

My daughter killed Mason.

'No, this can't be right,' I say, and I begin turning the pages some more, looking for any more details that might suggest Amber was just joking with what she said or that it was all just the ramblings of a vivid imagination. But the fact she knew about us being the ones who abducted Mason tells me she must have followed us, and, as I think about the logistics of it, I realise it actually could have happened.

I thought Amber and Jacob were still in bed when I left the house that morning to go and meet Guy at the spot where we would abduct Mason. But she could have been awake, and I guess she could have followed me in her car. I was more than a little distracted that morning with what I was about to do, so I wasn't exactly paying much attention to which cars were behind me as I made my way around town. The same goes for when I got to the warehouse and, by the sounds of it, Amber parked in a place where we couldn't see her even if we had been looking for anyone.

So she was the one who swooped in and killed Mason while we were stood outside the warehouse debating what to do with the prisoner?

But if so, how did she beat us home?

I think back to that fateful day and remember Guy getting us stuck in a traffic jam caused by temporary traffic lights and roadworks. He'd gone a different way than I would have thought he would, all because he was worried about CCTV cameras on our normal route, but that delay could have given Amber a chance to beat us back home.

The more I think about it, the more I see my daughter might actually have done what she says in her diary. But why write it down? And what if the police were to get hold of this?

The thought of a detective reading through these pages is a terrifying one, but I'm not done with reading it myself, because I realise this diary might hold the key to the one remaining mystery in all of this.

Sure enough, it does.

I only just got back before Mum and Dad, but when I made it up to my bedroom, I saw Dad carrying the ropes that Mason had been tied up with. He went around the back of the house with them so I couldn't see where he was putting them, but later that day, while everyone else was busy, I went outside and hunted around.

I found the ropes in the bin. The bin! How could Dad be so careless, especially when one of the ropes had blood on it! I knew he could clean the knife but those ropes were a problem. That's why I did what I did.

I took the ropes from the bin and put them in my car, figuring I'd dispose of them properly on my way back to university and then they definitely would not be found and get Mum and Dad in trouble. But as I was putting the ropes in my car, Erica Atkinson arrived, surprising me. She told me she'd heard I was back from university and wanted to say hello but then she saw the ropes and I panicked. I tried to cover them up but she knew something was wrong and when she asked me what was going on, I told her.

'Oh my god,' I say out loud to myself as I keep reading, unable to comprehend that Amber could have not only moved the ropes but ended up telling Erica Atkinson what they had been used for. But I have to keep reading because, so far, I still don't know how those ropes ended up in Kevin Atkinson's garage.

After breaking down in tears, the shock of the last few hours hitting me suddenly, I told Erica what I'd seen and done. But she didn't react how I thought she would. Instead of being shocked, she just smiled and said good riddance, clearly happy that Mason Burton was dead. She even thanked me and said she wanted to thank Mum and Dad too! But I told her she had to promise to stay quiet and she said she would, which I kind of knew she would do anyway because she hated Mason even more than we did. After composing myself, I told her I was going to get rid of the ropes, and she said she wanted to help me

*then, saying she would do it for me because my family had
already done enough for them by getting rid of Mason. So she
helped. She took the ropes for me.*

My hands are physically shaking as I hold the diary and
turn the page to read the next entry.

*I'm back at uni now and I think this is over. Erica told me she
buried the ropes in the woods and that should be the end of it.
It'll be our little secret. Two old friends who had drifted apart
over the last few years. But I guess we're still closer than I
thought.*

Erica buried the ropes in the woods? If they were buried
there, how did they end up in the garage? And then Amber's
next diary entry enlightens me.

*Oh my god. Jacob just phoned me and told me that the police
had just been at the house with a search warrant and had
raided all the rooms! They suspect Mum and Dad!*

My breathing is shallow as I read on, the sounds of laughter
from outside in the pool in stark contrast to the nightmare
unfolding in this hotel room.

*I'm scared that the police are going to arrest Mum and Dad for
Mason's death. I can't let them go to prison. I have to do
something.*

Why couldn't you just stay out of this? What the hell did
you do, Amber?

The next diary entry answers that question.

I called Erica and told her I was afraid Mum and Dad were going to be arrested. But she told me she was already worried about that too and had an idea. It was a crazy one and I tried to talk her out of it but she wanted to help us. She felt she owed us for getting rid of Mason. So she told me her plan.

'No,' I say as I nervously turn the page, but I already know what is coming. And sadly for me, I am right.

She was going to dig up the ropes and put them in her garage at home, which sounded crazy to me, but she told me the police wouldn't leave my family alone unless they had something else to look at. I told her she couldn't make her own family suspects, but she said they always would be anyway because of what Mason had done to Zoe. But at least in the case of the Atkinsons, they all had a good alibi for the time Mason died. All three of them were out of town, miles away in Cardiff, so Erica told me that even when the police found the rope and arrested Kevin, assuming he had done it, it would be impossible for a jury to say it was him or any other Atkinson because it was physically impossible for them to have been at the warehouse around that time. I told Erica she was crazy and not to do it, but she didn't listen, just thanking me again for what I'd done and promising this would all be over soon.

I turn the pages even quicker now, my heavy breathing drowning out the sounds from the other side of this hotel room window. As I read the next entry, I learn that Erica called Amber and explained how she had told her father what had happened, and he had agreed to go along with the plan. It seemed that while myself, Guy and Amber were struggling to keep our emotions under control in those early few days after what happened with Mason, the Atkinsons were far more composed and, apparently, Erica told Amber that was because they had spent three years processing what Mason had done to them as well as fantasising about what they would do to him if they only had the guts to. It seemed we had taken the revenge they only wished they could have taken and, once we had, they felt they could stand up to any attention from the police far easier than we could, which I guess they were right about.

There is one more entry from Amber on this matter, and I am crying as I read it.

> *I feel so anxious waiting to see what happens to Kevin but Erica insists everything will be okay and no jury will ever convict her dad. For now, I know I need to move on, and my family can do the same. I love them so much. I just want them to be safe. They were just protecting bro. I was just protecting them. And now Erica and her father are going to protect us.*

Tears run down my cheeks as I discover the full extent of just how much Amber loves her family, and the crazy lengths she has gone to in order to keep us all out of danger.

But now that I know, what shall I do about it?

My first thought is to rush down to the pool and tell Guy, but how will he react? And surely, we have to confront our daughter about this, but what will happen when we do? And how could we ever hope to keep any of it a secret from Jacob?

There are far too many uncertainties, and they are the last thing I need when my daughter is a killer, and we inadvertently assisted her in that crime.

Still clutching the diary tightly, I leave Amber's room and cross through the living area, past the sofa bed, before unlocking the sliding doors and stepping out onto the sun-drenched balcony. Looking down from my high vantage point, I see my family by the pool. Guy is still sipping his beer, Jacob is still splashing around in the water and his sister is right there beside him, enjoying the pool too.

They all look so happy, so content.

Just how I was ten minutes ago before I came up here and read this diary.

It's in that moment that I know what to do with it.

I am going to destroy it so no one else can ever read it and learn the horrifying things that are contained within the pages.

Most of all, I am going to protect Amber, just like she protected me.

But what about when she notices that her diary is missing? Will she panic and think it's fallen into the wrong hands? I suppose she would, so before I rip the pages to shreds and destroy all the evidence, I go back into Amber's room and use her pen to write a short message on a blank page that I tear out and place by her bed.

It's a simple message and one she will understand when she sees it later. After finishing writing it, I leave her room and make good on my promise to myself to destroy the diary, tearing out the pages with the ink on them, ripping them to shreds and, finally, flushing it all down the toilet. Only then do I leave the hotel room and go back downstairs to join my family out in the sun again. But the message I wrote remains inside, in the shadows, waiting to be read before it, too, will be ripped up like the diary.

Amber, darling.

Revenge is sweet; there is no doubt about that, but what is even sweeter is making sure you get away with it. That's what I have just ensured. We need to talk but not until we are home. Try and enjoy the rest of the holiday.

Love you lots,

Mum xxx

. . .

Finding my family exactly where I had left them before I went to the hotel room and made a shocking discovery, it takes me a little while before I can consider myself to be back in the holiday spirit. But as the afternoon wears on and the four of us continue to bask beneath a revitalising sun, the shock wears off and I see that Amber only did the same thing as I did.

I'd do anything to protect my family and that's exactly what I just did.

All that matters is their safety and their safety is now assured.

I'm not a bad person for doing that and there would have been no need to get revenge if those who did wrong hadn't done wrong in the first place.

I'm glad it's over now.

I'm not sure I could go through all of that again.

Or maybe I could.

It's surprising how far a parent will go to save their child.

It's also just as surprising to learn how far a child will go to save their parent.

A LETTER FROM DANIEL

Dear reader,

I want to say a huge thank you for choosing to read *The Couple's Revenge*. If you did enjoy it and would like to keep up to date with all my latest releases, please sign up at the following link. Your email address will never be shared and you can unsubscribe at any time.

www.bookouture.com/daniel-hurst

I hope you loved *The Couple's Revenge* and if you did, I would be very grateful if you could write an honest review. I'd love to hear what you think, and it makes such a difference in helping new readers to discover my books for the first time.

I also love hearing from my readers, and you can get in touch with me directly at my email address daniel@danielhurst books.com. I reply to every message! You can also visit my website where you can download a free psychological thriller called 'Just One Second'.

Thank you,

Daniel

KEEP IN TOUCH WITH DANIEL

www.danielhurstbooks.com

facebook.com/danielhurstbooks

instagram.com/danielhurstbooks

Made in United States
Orlando, FL
31 March 2024

45297118R00146